YOURS TO GIVE

LANTERN BAY, BOOK 1

SOPHIE HAYDON

BAY BOOKS

Yours to Give
by Sophie Haydon

A dare, a marriage, a happily ever after?

—The Mackenzies—
A Place Called Home
Secrets at Parata Bay
Escape to Shelter Springs
What you See in the Stars
Second Chance at Whisper Creek
Summer at the Lakehouse Café

—Lantern Bay—
Yours to Give
Yours to Treasure
Yours to Cherish
Yours to Keep
Yours Forever
Yours to Love

For more information about this author, visit:
https://sophiehaydon.com

© 2017 Diana Fraser

ISBN: 978-1-99-102113-7 (2022 Amazon print edn)
ISBN: 978-1-99-102130-4 (2022 Draft2Digital print edn)

CONTENTS

"It is during our darkest moments that we must focus to see the light."
— **Aristotle**

"LAURA'S ARRIVED IN NEW ZEALAND!
WHAT'S HER NEXT CHALLENGE? WATCH
THIS SPACE!!" @TELLTALEGIRL
#NUMBERONEFAN

*M*ax Connelly narrowed his eyes against the bright sunlight and gave a long low whistle as a young woman tore by on a state-of-the-art mountain bike. She wore ripped jeans and a tiny top. Strands of long blonde hair escaped her safety helmet and flew behind her as she hurtled at breakneck speed down the steep grassy slope. Within seconds she'd reached the edge of the bluff and flew off, into the air.

Max held his breath like everyone else around him, waiting to see if she and her bike would part ways. Only the most experienced bikers ever attempted that jump. As she landed with a thud and a wobble, there was a collective outrush of amazement. But she didn't stop. Instead, she hurtled along the ridge, either side of which precipitous cliffs plunged.

Max gripped the balustrade of the terrace and cursed under his breath. Surely she wouldn't risk everything merely to get to the edge—a challenge reserved for only the most extreme sporting aficionados. At the last moment she twisted the bike around. Dust flew up around her as she jammed on her brakes and came to an abrupt halt at the very edge of the drop.

She gave a whoop of exultation and Max grinned—partly sharing her excitement and partly in relief. Her infectious laughter filled the small valley as she jumped off the bike and went to join her friends.

Without looking away from the woman, he placed his drink on the table and leaned over the balustrade of the Lodge's wide terrace, shaking his head in disbelief. "Did you see her? Man, she can move!"

"Max!" He looked around to find his sister, Lizzi, grinning at him. "Is that the owner's perk—checking out young women?"

"Who is she?" Max asked, ignoring her question. "An actress or model or something?"

"No idea. Whoever she is, she's popular. Looks like she's got quite a circle of admirers." Lizzi laughed. "Good luck with that one, bro!"

Max's eyes strayed back to the woman who'd unclipped her helmet and was shaking out her blonde hair. Like everyone else, he couldn't take his eyes off her.

The bright light seemed to emanate from her like an aura, but he knew it was more likely the effect of them being over five thousand feet up in the Southern Alps.

She was gorgeous. She was also either courageous or stupid—he didn't know which but he decided then and there he'd find out. And there was something else, another quality, which was totally disarming. She moved with an ease and unselfconsciousness, as if she had no clue how truly compelling she was. She tossed her helmet to someone and now stood, hands on slender hips, legs slightly apart. Not *girly* feminine, but definitely attractive. *Very* attractive.

"That's Laura McKinney," said Rachel, one of his other sisters who he'd managed to persuade to join him at his summer party at the mountain lodge. "She's the new YouTube sensation. She accepts dares and films them as she goes. She's quite something. Haven't you come across her? She's the darling of the media in the US. She's over here for a few weeks."

"In Queenstown? For a few weeks?" Max turned to Rachel. "How come I haven't heard of this?"

Rachel rolled her eyes. "An oversight of your staff, I'm sure."

"My staff managed to get *you* here. That's a near miracle." He frowned. "How did they manage to tear you away from Wellington, anyway?" It was as if a cloud descended on Rachel and she looked away. Max looked across at Lizzi to see if she was aware of a change in Rachel, but Lizzi was in a world of her own since she'd met Pete. He was glad but it didn't help him any. He made a mental note to find out what was bothering Rachel. But not now. Later. He looked back at the vision below him. "So how come they didn't tell me about the famous Laura McKinney? She could be good for business."

Rachel rested her folded arms on the railing and looked up at him. His first instinct was correct. Something *had* unsettled Rachel. He could see it in her eyes but before he could ask her what the matter was a cheer went up as waiters, carrying bottles of Champagne, approached Laura and the crowd which had gathered around her.

"Laura doesn't *do* planning. She arrives, she surprises, and then she's gone again. I doubt even Chelsey knew about Laura's intentions."

"Huh," grunted Max. "I pay her to know this kind of stuff."

"Why are you so annoyed?"

"Because that's the whole point of the summer party—to raise the Lodge's profile, to draw visitors to it—both summer and winter. That's why I have a PR team." He huffed an irritated sigh. "And, besides, I've made arrangements to leave for Australia in a couple of days."

"Ah, I get it," said Rachel. "Now you've seen Laura, you'd prefer to hang out here, rather than enjoy Sydney's high life. Although, seriously, Max, I don't think Laura is your type."

Max frowned. "And what's my type?"

Rachel and Lizzi exchanged knowing glances. "You know. Super sophisticated, wealthy types. Jimmy Choo shoes, Birkin handbags, Ray-Ban sunglasses."

Max's frown deepened. "None of that means anything to me."

"No, but the type of women wearing them do."

"Give up, Rachel," said Lizzi. "He's a lost cause."

But Max was oblivious to their teasing and continued to watch the blonde below the terrace.

"You won't get anywhere there, Max, so I wouldn't even bother," said Rachel.

The idea of a woman turning him down was a new one to Max. "Why? Doesn't she like men?"

"Oh, she likes them all right. Likes them enough to insist that she'll never go out with anyone longer than a month. She's publicly stated that long-term relationships are for idiots and marriage is ridiculous."

"My kind of girl, then."

Rachel laughed and shook her head.

"See you later," said Max, descending the steps towards the blonde.

LAURA BREATHED DEEPLY of the fresh clear air, sucking it into her lungs, feeding the blood that surged through her veins. She lived for moments like these. Her perceptions were always intensely heightened after a challenge—a result of the adrenaline she assumed. Whatever it was, she needed that rush more than food or water.

She glanced at the jump she'd leaped off and grinned. It looked impossible from this angle. Just as well she hadn't seen it from this angle then. But she knew she'd still have done it. Doing the impossible gave her an even bigger thrill.

"You're crazy, Laura!" shouted her best friend and manager, Kelly, who handed her a bottle of Champagne. One of the men tried to take it from her to prize off the cork, but Laura held onto it.

"Maybe." She turned to the man and pulled the bottle away from his hands, with a smile. "But if I can make that jump, I'm pretty sure I can take the cork out of a bottle of Champagne."

Cameras clicked and flashed all around as the Champagne exploded in her hands and she lifted the bottle to drink from its foaming neck. She tilted her head, looking up at the bright blue sky and the white-topped mountains and swallowed Champagne, as more spilled down the sides of the bottle and flowed onto her hand and arm. She'd never felt more alive. And that's what this was all about, wasn't it?

Choking slightly, she wiped her mouth on the back of her hand and looked up again as she heard a cry from above. She watched, mesmerized, as a large hawk flew directly overhead. For a strange moment she felt as if she *were* that hawk, looking down on them, all powerful, each beautiful wingtip responsive to the wind, adjusting, feeling, living, constantly moving. She could sense its vibrations in her own limbs.

The hawk sailed past on the air currents and Laura looked down, straight into a pair of eyes which held the same acute focus as the bird.

The eyes were narrowed in a tanned face, a strong face, and one which had an air of total authority. She didn't think he'd even noticed the other people around her. He was the kind of man who was supremely confident, able to avoid anything that wasn't of interest to him.

Seemed *she* was of interest to him. She swallowed and licked her lips. There was no man she liked better than a confident one.

"Hi!" She smiled and passed the bottle to someone, without shifting her gaze from the stranger.

"Hi!" There was a silence between them which was all she could hear, despite the clamor, shouts and laughter of the people all around her. He glanced down at her Champagne-soaked t-shirt that stopped short of her pierced belly button. She didn't mind being looked at. She was used to it after seven years of traveling the world in search of new challenges. And she particularly didn't mind his look of appreciation. So long as it stayed at that. She dressed for herself, not for anyone else. She'd always hated to feel restricted by clothes. If a side-effect was that men liked to look at her, she didn't mind. She could look after herself.

"That was quite some jump," he said, but she could see that his eyes held an interest in more than just the jump. It was reinforced by the smile that told her that he was thinking quite different thoughts.

"Sure was. That was the whole reason I came here."

"Is that right? Not to see our beautiful country, the Southern Alps, the oceans, the fiords, the beaches?"

She could listen to him talk forever. There was something in his macho Kiwi accent that tugged at her in a place it really shouldn't. He was saying one thing, but her body was responding as if he was running his hand up her arms, and curving his fingers around her neck, stroking her. *Get a grip!*

"I'm sure they're all amazing, but it's not what I'm in to."

"And what are you in to?"

"Thrills and spills."

"I'm glad you didn't spill."

"That's kind."

"No, it's not. I own this place and if you'd spilled, it could have dragged me down, too."

Laura wasn't fazed by his rebuke. There was humor in his tone and his eyes still held that interested light which took the edge off his words. "I wouldn't have wanted to drag you down."

"Come to think of it, it might have been interesting."

The electric buzz of attraction fizzed in the pit of her stomach. If she loved adrenaline, the double buzz of lust *and* adrenaline was a sure-fire winner. She stepped forward and drew her hand down his arm. "Would hate to have had that lovely shirt dirtied in the process, though."

She smiled as his eyes narrowed even more, in a way that made her stomach flutter with desire. She could just imagine the thoughts going around his brain, and his body. "I don't mind getting dirty, darlin'. Just say the word."

She gave a throaty laugh and stepped away. His expression didn't change. She had him where she wanted him—*if* she wanted him.

"Hey, Laura!" She glanced around to see Rachel Connelly put her arm around the stranger. "I see you've met my big brother, Max."

Max looked from one to the other. "You two know each other?"

Laura grinned. "Rach and I met in Wellington a few months ago. She invited me onto her cooking show. I didn't do so bad, did I, Rach?"

Rach grimaced. "Not so good, either. I didn't see *you* eating anything you made."

"I'd only have done that if there'd been a challenge attached." She looked back at Max. "So this is your big brother you were telling me about."

"You been talking about me, Rachel?"

"Yep." Rachel grinned, obviously enjoying his discomfort.

"Nothing bad I hope," said Max.

"Nothing good, or else I wouldn't have been interested," said Laura.

"So that means you *are* interested?" he asked.

"Maybe. Although the way Rachel described you I thought you'd be, I'm not sure, *meaner* looking somehow."

"Rachel," said Max in a low growl as he glared at his sister. "What have you been saying about me?"

"Only that you're my bossy big brother, who thinks he knows best in every situation. You don't let anyone or anything stand in your way—business or pleasure."

"So basically a ruthless bastard then."

"That about sums it up." Rachel shrugged. "Oh, and I might have said that you change women like you change jackets."

He shrugged. "Seasons change, needs change."

"Good point," said Laura. "Sometimes, it's warm and you like something light and easy. And sometimes, it's cold, and you need something hotter."

"My point exactly. You see, Rachel." Max didn't take his eyes off Laura. "Laura and I have a lot more in common than you thought."

Rachel looked from one to the other. "Maybe you're right. What do you reckon, Laura?"

Laura shrugged, not wanting to admit that she reckoned she and Max had a whole *lot* in common. Max looked pretty confident, pretty sure of himself. She had an urge to put a dent in that sureness. "Well, we both dress to the season. But then so do millions of others. So… I don't know. I'd have to know more about your big brother before I made a decision on that point."

"I'm sure my big brother won't be unhappy to get to know you better."

Laura stood beside Rachel pretending to consider Max whose brow lowered in irritation. "I'm not sure if your big brother is looking very happy now."

"I'm sure he is." Rachel wrinkled up her nose. "He pretends he doesn't like being talked about but he does. It massages his macho ego."

Laura grinned. "Still not looking happy."

"I will be when you stop talking about me as if I weren't here," growled Max.

"Aww, Max, don't be grouchy," said Rachel, linking her arm through his. "It's only because we love you."

"*I* don't love him," Laura pointed out.

"Oh, you will," said Rachel with complete confidence. "Everyone loves Max." She thought for a second. "At least they do while he loves them. Happily, he loves his family, even if he doesn't show it."

Max shook his head. "God knows why I love my family when they're such pains in the ass."

There was a shout and Rachel glanced up to the Lodge. "It's Lizzi. Looks like lunch is ready. Coming, Laura?"

"I'd love to, but I've a TV crew waiting in Queenstown to interview me." Laura stepped toward Max, unable to stop flirting. It was fun seeing a macho man on the wrong side of the balance of power for once. "But maybe I'll see you at dinner, Max?"

He didn't move, only shifted his eyes to look at her as she stepped away with a smile. "Oh, you will. I'll make sure of it."

"Maybe we can discover if we have anything else in common other than changing jackets according to season?"

She left before he could answer.

"DAMN, DAMN, DAMN, DAMN, DAMN!"

Chelsey Jones, Max's marketing manager, paced away from Max toward the window, but Max knew she wasn't admiring the view. She stood with her hands on her suited hips, blonde hair smoothed into a French twist, as elegant as ever, but unusually disconcerted.

"Damn!" she added for good luck before turning back to Max. "They made the booking under another name. I had no idea."

"Rachel tells me Laura and her team are out of here the day after tomorrow." He tapped a finger irritably on the wooden armrest of the couch. "If only we'd known we could have capitalized on her visit with some publicity of our own."

She shook her head. "I know. I'm sorry, Max. I dropped the ball. I should have been on to it as soon as they arrived. But I was in Wanaka and…"

As irritated as he was that they'd let the opportunity slip through their fingers, Max couldn't stay angry with Chelsey for long. They went back a long way and, from the slight droop of her shoulders, he could see she was more angry with herself. "That's okay. Everyone's entitled to time off."

She turned to face him, her expression stern. "No, it's not all right. If I'd only known I could have arranged some meetings… a few situations to showcase the Lodge and all it has to offer. I could have done what you employed me to do—make Queenstown Lodge *the* place to be in the Southern Hemisphere."

He rose and went to her and laid his hand on her tense shoulders. "Chill, it's okay." He lifted her chin so she was forced to face him. "But tell me…"

She frowned. "Yes?"

"Why only the Southern Hemisphere?"

She smiled and stood straighter. "Because your ego needs to be contained, Max Connelly." She paced away from Max once more, tapping her cellphone against her lips.

Max sighed. It was always a bad sign when Chelsey was deep in thought. It usually meant work for him. She turned and caught his gaze.

"What can we do to keep her here?" she asked.

He shrugged. "She doesn't strike me as the sort of person you can keep anywhere."

"If you can make her stay for at least a week, that'll give me time to get some national media attention."

"She's on YouTube all the time. Won't that do?"

"Not by itself. We need to get you two together, engage the media, and get them pointing to Laura's YouTube channel, and it should snowball from there."

"Me and Laura. Together."

"You know what I mean. Judging by the video clips from this afternoon, it's not going to be hard for either of you."

"You think a little flirtation would be good for business." He didn't phrase it as a question. He knew it was what they were both thinking. He also felt unaccountably ill at ease with the idea.

"Don't tell me you have qualms about that, because I won't believe you. Business *always* comes first with you."

"You know me so well."

She walked up to him, and tapped her cellphone on his chest. "Yes, I do."

She looked up at him with a wistfulness which disarmed him. He'd called off their relationship a year ago and he didn't think he'd ever be able to do enough to recompense for the hurt he'd caused her—a hurt that rarely showed through. He'd thought he saw a glimpse of it now, but it was too quickly gone to be sure.

"I'll get in contact with Kelly, Laura's PA," Chelsey continued. "If she's as smart an operator as I think she is, she'll see the benefit in staying around for another week. Leave it with me. You go and flirt outrageously with Laura and I'll do the rest."

"You're using me for my hunky appeal, Chelsey."

She rolled her eyes. "Don't tell me you don't like it."

"True," he said, walking toward the door. "We all have to play to our strengths."

He closed the door on Chelsey's groan.

MAX'S MEETING with Chelsey had made him late for dinner. He took a short cut along the front terrace, noting the old lantern hanging, unlit, by the entrance. Most people assumed it to be a broken antique, there for its charm alone. But in his grandparents' day it had worked. His grandmother had said it was a guide in the darkness to bring friends and family home. It was a tradition his mother had brought to his family home in Akaroa—and one he'd let slip. He closed his eyes briefly as grief at losing his late mother hit him afresh. When he could bear to think of his mother's passing without pain, he'd fix the lantern, not before.

He paused on the threshold of the restaurant and looked around. The place was packed with Lodge guests and casual diners enjoying the finest wines and food prepared by the French chef he'd persuaded to move here. The chandeliers glittered overhead, sparking light from the crystal glassware. The concertina windows were pushed back to allow the cool night air into the warm room.

He was proud of the Lodge, what it had been, and what it had become. He'd built on the old-fashioned charm of the original Lodge, keeping its character but bringing it into the twenty-first century. But his ambitions for it hadn't stopped —not by a long way.

A quick scan revealed Rachel sitting next to Laura, surrounded by others. Ignoring Rachel's knowing grin, he walked over, persuaded the person sitting on Laura's other side to leave with the lure of free wine, and took the place himself.

"Mind if I join you?"

"And what if I say no?" said Laura.

"Then you'll have to inform the owner who, I'm afraid, has my best interests at heart."

"Maybe I will," she said, sitting back, an eyebrow raised in query. "What do you think he'll do about it?"

He flashed a quick smile at the waitress who set a new place for him. "Probably tell you that you should reconsider."

"Really? And why should I?" She leaned in toward him, flirtatiously. "Is he such great company? Is he so utterly charming, witty, and interesting?"

Max raised his eyebrows. "He's all that but, more importantly, he'll sulk if you don't let him sit beside you. And you really don't want to see a grown man sulk."

Laura laughed, a laugh that wrapped around inside him and gave a sharp tug. It was adorable—strangely natural and innocent for all her worldliness and flirtatious, danger-seeking nature. "You're right. I don't. You'd better make yourself comfortable then."

Max signaled the waiter who brought him a plate of hors d'oeuvres. He helped himself as a wine waiter poured him a large glass of his favorite Central Otago pinot noir. "So how are you enjoying Queenstown?"

"It's wonderful. It has everything I love here. Extreme sports, beautiful scenery, but with an airport so you can escape to the city if you want to. I could live here."

"You should."

"No, I won't. What I mean is, if I had another job, another personality, another life, I could live here." She shook her head. "But I don't settle."

"I can understand that. I only returned here a year ago after traveling pretty much constantly overseas."

"What did you do?"

"Everything. Made money through various businesses. Tried my hand at different things."

"Successful?"

"Yep. Made enough to buy this place and some other properties in the area."

"So why come back?"

Max didn't speak immediately. He drank from his glass and put it down carefully on the table before turning to her. "I'd had enough. I wanted to stop, spend time with my family, my friends. I wanted to know them. I wanted to know *this* place. After a while, traveling becomes tedious. You must find that."

Laura looked uncomfortable. "Not really. I find it exciting. Besides, I like to keep things simple. And it's simpler to keep moving."

He raised his eyebrows in surprise. "That sounds kind of... restless." She didn't respond. "You don't find that way of life lonely at all?"

"Are you kidding me? I'm always surrounded by people."

He looked around. "And you're close to all these people?"

Whether it was the way he'd asked the question, or the question itself, something made her pause. Her green eyes flickered over his and he could see enticing glimpses of doubt behind the bravado. Bravado was alluring, but doubt was intriguing.

"No," she said. "Only a couple of them. The rest are"—she shrugged—"just there. That's enough for me."

"Really?" he asked gently, his curiosity piqued by her response. "And I thought *I* liked a minimalist life."

She raised an eyebrow and indicated all around with her

glass of soda water. "Minimalist? With all this? You're kidding me!"

"Good point. This is probably the least minimalist part of my life. I came here with some mates a year ago and, once I'd seen this place again, I couldn't let it go."

"You fell in love with it." She looked around. "I'm not surprised—it's a wonderful place."

"Oh, I'd fallen for it over thirty years ago." He smiled at her confusion. "You see, it belonged to my grandparents. My mother used to bring me here as a youngster to get me away from my dad."

Laura shot him an interested look. "You don't get on with your dad?"

"No. Still don't. Anyhow, this place meant more to me growing up than my own home. My grandparents died while I was overseas and it was left to a cousin of mine. Mum had passed away by then and Dad wasn't interested. But when I came back here the place was falling into ruin." He shook his head. "I couldn't walk away from it."

"So you bought it off your cousin?"

"Yeah. He was relieved. He had no interest in it and had been trying to sell it for years. But it needed a lot of money pouring into it."

"So… you poured the money in and you've made a wonderful place. But…" She hesitated.

"Go on," Max prompted. "Ask away."

"But why? I wouldn't have taken you for the sentimental type. And you're so far away from most other countries it must be hard to keep it commercially viable."

Max didn't answer immediately. Was he sentimental? He'd never thought of himself like that but it was true, he'd done it because, somewhere deep down, he'd heard his mother's voice saying it was the right thing to do. He'd always been guided by that voice because it had never failed him.

"I'm *not* sentimental. I do what I think is right. Simple as that. And it's going just fine. *And* we have plans. Big plans."

"You're going to make your grandparents proud."

He nodded. And his mother. Though he wasn't going to tell Laura that. She might call him sentimental again and he had an image to maintain.

"They'd be pleased. It was *the* holiday place to come to in the 1920s, when my great-grandparents ran it. And if you think it's out of the way now, you should have tried to get here then. It took a week to get here from Christchurch and half of that was from Cromwell, where the rail line ended. It was a challenge all right."

"One I'd have been up for." She grinned.

He smiled back. "You know? I can just imagine you here, in the middle of last century, clipping on your wooden skis, trekking out to get wood for the fire."

"Right. I get the picture. You see me as some kind of pioneer, a colonial woman come to claim her place in the world. I'd have liked everything except the claiming part. I don't want to claim anything for my own."

"Looks pretty much like you've claimed the world if the number of views on YouTube are anything to go by."

She raised her chin. "You've been checking me out online." She grunted softly. He liked the sound.

"Simply keeping myself informed about my visitors."

She pushed away her empty plate and sat back in her chair, nursing her glass of soda water, and shot him a challenging look. "So tell me, what have you learned about me?"

"I'm pretty sure you know what I've learned about you. Your life is an open book. But I can read between the lines," he said, unable to resist teasing her.

"Between the lines? Nothing there but empty white space, I should imagine."

"Should you? Then you'd be wrong." He paused, intrigued by the flash of doubt which lurked behind her eyes—darker, more mysterious now. He liked mystery, and he also liked women.

Her phone beeped and she picked it up. "Excuse me." She rose and walked outside. He watched her as she went and realized he wasn't alone. Those diners who hadn't moved to the bar next door, were glancing her way. She had that knack of making people look at her, without revealing a shred of self-consciousness.

She returned to the table, sliding the phone onto it, and cocked her head to one side. "So, it seems Kelly wants me to extend our stay a week. Kelly and your marketing manager believe it'll be good for business."

"You okay with that?"

"Is there enough around here to keep me occupied for a week?"

"I'm sure of it. Lots of things to explore. Lots of attractions."

"Is that right?"

"I can guarantee you'll enjoy yourself."

"Well"—she rose out of her chair and turned, arms crossed under her perfectly formed breasts—"in that case, how can I refuse?" Without waiting for a response, she turned and walked across the room, toward the door. "Goodnight," she called without turning around.

"Goodnight." He watched her walk, barefoot, along the wooden veranda, her long blonde hair skimming her back and shoulders. His gaze dropped to her rear, perfectly enhanced by the worn jeans.

This was going to be an interesting week.

2

"WHO'S THAT MAN FLIRTING WITH LAURA?
AND, MORE IMPORTANTLY, WHAT'S SHE
GOING TO DO ABOUT IT?" @TELLTALEGIRL
#ROMANCEISINTHEAIR

There was no sign of Laura the next morning which was just as well. It meant he could focus, or at least try to focus on his other guests, and his family. He adored spending time with his little niece, Aimee, which he and Rachel purposely did, giving the newly loved-up Lizzi time with his good mate, Pete. He really wanted it to work out for them.

But, as much as he enjoyed being with Aimee, he couldn't help glancing over his shoulder whenever he heard a shout, or a group of people approach. Because he'd worked out that Laura was never alone, her entrance was always heralded by an excited buzz of voices and laughter. He wondered whether her need for company extended to the bedroom. Despite her flirtatious nature, there were no scandals surrounding her, no talk of lovers, spurned or otherwise.

After lunch he and Rachel waved off his sister, Lizzi, Pete and Aimee before returning to the Lodge's terrace. Rachel's phone rang and she tapped it, and glanced up at Max with a heartbreaking expression of sadness and anger. The phone stopped ringing and she sighed with relief. But before she could slip it back into her pocket, a text came through. She read it, grunted with anger and tossed the phone onto the table. It landed with a clatter.

"Not in the mood for a phone call?"

She turned to him with surprise, her expression grim. "You could say that."

"Want to talk about it?"

"Not sure there's much point."

"Try it and we'll see if a point eventuates."

She shrugged. "My latest fling. Except I didn't realize it was only a fling until now. I don't know why I always end up with men I work with."

"Cameraman or director?"

"Cameraman," she said with a sigh. "I held such high hopes for him. Turned out the reason he wanted that revealing photo of me was to put it on his Facebook page."

"Bastard! What's his name?" Max was incensed.

She patted his arm. "Thank you, big brother. But you can't go and sort it out like you used to in the playground."

"Want to bet?" Max was ready to jump onto the next plane and make sure this pathetic individual was never able to upset his sister again.

"No, actually I don't. But I don't want you to do anything. I've dealt with it."

Max grunted and turned to look at the view, his gaze narrowed as he wondered, not for the first time, why his gorgeous sisters—both Rachel and Lizzi—had such trouble with men. It wasn't because they weren't strong. They managed to sort him out all right.

"Did you fire him?" he asked.

"Yep."

"So at least he won't be there when you get back to Wellington."

"I'm not sure I'm going back to Wellington. This is just one time too many. I need a change."

"From your TV show? But you've worked so hard on that. Built it up from nothing." Max couldn't imagine his little sister, who'd been dubbed New Zealand's answer to Nigella Lawson, doing anything different.

"No, I'm not going to give up my career. But I may take it some place else. I've had approaches from the US."

"Cool."

"Yeah. But there's a few issues to iron out so I'm going to head home to Belendroit for a while before going overseas. I haven't spent any length of time there for years."

"Dad will appreciate your company. Not sure how long you'll be able to stand it though, not after the excitement of your show-biz life in Wellington."

"At the moment a non-show-biz life, hundreds of miles from Wellington, sounds pretty damn good. At least for a while."

"Then do it."

She glanced at her phone and nodded. "I think I will." She gave him a hug and chucked him under the chin. His sisters were the only people he'd ever accept that from. "You don't mind if I clear out early?"

"Do what you have to do. How long do you think you'll stay in Akaroa?"

"I'm not sure. There are a few things I want to do there— six months tops."

He watched her walk away. "Call me!"

Rachel waved a hand of acknowledgement. "Sure thing."

Suddenly a phone rang and he looked down. It was Rachel's. He picked it up, still unlocked from her previous conversation, and looked into the face of the caller. Max cleared his throat and prepared to put the fear of God into Rachel's ex.

Satisfied that Rachel wouldn't be bothered by her ex anymore, Max returned to his office. His sanctuary.

Chelsey teased him about it—called his style 'grunge-minimalist'. He didn't mind, she could call it whatever she wanted, so long as she didn't try to prettify anything. One old couch placed in front of an open fire, an over-sized screen, and fridge and other gadgets hidden behind a bank of seamless doors, was all there was. It was enough.

He didn't want distractions. He had work to do. He'd taken on this place with one aim only—to bring his mother's old home back to life, to make her proud, to remember her. And to do that, he intended to make it a huge success.

Other people might assume he was driven by money, and he was to some extent, but that wasn't the whole story. But he didn't want people to know the whole story.

He put his feet up on his office couch, one of the few things he'd kept from his grandparents' days. The orangey-brown material was worn on the arms—it even had stuffing coming out. A single piece of nostalgia. Everyone should have at least one, he reckoned.

He flicked a remote, entered Laura's name, pressed play and lay back to watch a re-run of yesterday's mountain bike stunt.

Laura's face filled the whole screen, revealing just how nervous she was. She spoke a few words and then let her sunglasses drop onto her nose, took a deep breath, and pushed off down the hill. There was one long cry and then silence as Max saw her grip tighten on the handles—her focus complete. She skilfully maneuvered the course, but even her obvious experience didn't prevent her from hitting some of the obstacles full on, forcing her to readjust, challenging her on every level.

It was a professional recording of her descent from the peak with various cameras positioned along the route, each taking up where the other left off. Max was impressed. Not least with the woman herself.

Rachel had got it partly right. He *was* interested. But as to her not being his type, his two sisters, Rachel and Lizzi, were quite wrong there. Laura McKinney was *exactly* his type. Not interested in marriage, not interested in children, but *very* interested in fun.

Max put his feet on the arm of the couch, his arms behind his head, pressed the pause button, and gazed at the lovely Laura McKinney just as she reached the bottom of the slope, her face frozen in sheer relief and joy. If that was how she looked after she'd experienced the thrill and landed, he wanted to see that face, close up and personal.

He swung his legs off the couch and entered the address of her Twitter feed. He wanted to know what she was doing and where she was doing it. He soon found his answer. He jumped up and stood in front of the large screen. First he looked at her photograph—laughing, her smile lighting up her face, her hair swept back as she was caught, mid-flight, on some contraption or other. He shook his head and checked the hashtags. What next? #bungyjump. He should have known. He made a note of which operator she was going to, switched the screen off, and pulled his phone from his pocket.

She was a woman who liked challenges, and he had just the challenge for her.

AN HOUR later Max arrived at the river and met his friend.

They shook hands.

"Good of you to let me barge in."

"No problems, Max. It's not as if you haven't done the job many times before. Just make sure you don't stuff it up, though." He glanced up at the crowd of people on top of the bridge 140 feet above the raging river. "I don't want this to be the one challenge which breaks Laura McKinney."

"Nor do I, mate. Nor do I. I reckon we've worked often enough together that I could do this in my sleep." Their joint gazes watched as people milled around on the bridge. Only the occasional flash of blonde hair revealed Laura's presence.

Unnoticed by any of the crowds, his friend pushed the boat off into the river and Max steered it through the currents, pulling up in the lee of some rocks. Here he looked up, shading his eyes from the sun with his hands.

Laura had emerged and was standing on the platform ready to dive. Unlike the people who'd gone before, there was no one holding on to her. She'd waved people away as she stood up on the ledge. She hesitated but Max instinctively knew it wasn't from fear. She was born to live life in the limelight. She thrived on the public's response, she moved and responded to the crowds with every bone in her body. Flashes of camera and gasps emerged as they watched her raise her hands in the air. She even went on tiptoe for a few seconds. Max smiled. It was all for dramatic effect. She really knew how to wrap people around her little finger. Himself included. Maybe he was as bad as Rachel at being attracted to the wrong people.

Then a noise erupted—equal gasp, equal cheer—as she jumped off, and plummeted earthwards, the bungy rope fixed to her ankles unraveling behind her, like some giant snake following her to earth. Even Max, who'd witnessed more bungy jumps than he cared to remember, had his heart in his mouth as he watched her strong, lithe body hold itself firm against the rushing air, her hair streaming out like a bright flag behind her.

Max revved the engine and steered it into the middle of the Kawarau River just as Laura plummeted to earth. He was so close he could see her shut her eyes as she rushed headlong toward the water. She'd chosen to not stop short of the water, but to dive head first into the chill, glacier-fed river. A risky choice but for someone so young and fit, a calculated one. As usual she was dressed only in a brief white bikini, stunning against her tanned body. It seemed being practically naked in the eyes of the world didn't worry her.

She kept her arms crossed over her chest as she entered the water, the bungy rope stretching until only her ankles were visible for one instant before the rope rebounded and jerked her up, out of the water with a gasp, trailing a blast of bright sunlit water.

He expertly maneuvered the boat around, ready to pick her up. She gasped as she dangled there and then, with an agility which didn't surprise him, she swung herself up, catching hold of the rope and righting herself. With the instinct of a circus performer she held out her free arm and leg wide and swung around the rope in a picture of elegance and athleticism. Applause roared through the valley.

Slowly the winch lowered her until she was in the boat. He pulled his cap lower and helped her in, not that she needed it. She dropped in as if she'd jumped off a bus.

"Cheers!" she said to him with barely a glance before waving to her audience, both up on the bridge and on shore.

She sat down, braced her arms behind her and laughed, turning her bright face up to the sun. She was irresistible. There didn't seem to be anything between her and anyone else. Most people had built walls around them, layers of armor to protect themselves from hurt, from feeling, from a hundred other things which had been chucked their way in the course of their lives. Not Laura. It seemed she didn't need any armor—all she wanted was to feel alive.

He waited for her to give the signal.

"Okay, let's go!" she said.

He nodded, noting her GoPro camera was still filming,

checked his route and gunned the motor, tearing off downstream instead of back to shore.

She fell back into the boat with the force of the acceleration. Water splashed up, soaking them both.

"Hey! Where are we going?" she spluttered, as she pushed her wet hair from her face.

He grinned and glanced at her. For the first time she looked at him, *really* looked.

"You! What are you doing? Have you kidnapped me?"

"I thought you might appreciate a different kind of challenge to the predictable bungy jumping."

"But—"

He looked back to where he was going. "If I were you, I'd stop talking and hang on tight."

She screamed—half-panic and half-pleasure—as he took the rapids straight on, all four hundred meters of turbulent water. He'd done it plenty of times before and knew the lay of the rocks beneath the water like the back of his own hand. There was no danger but he'd somehow forgotten to tell her that.

Now out of sight of the curious onlookers, he continued on down the river until they came to a secluded spot. The cliffs soared high above them, turning into mountains. There were no roads around here, no access way, no one to see them. He spun the motor boat into a quiet inlet.

She turned the GoPro on herself. Max saw the red light blinking. "I can now add shooting the rapids and being kidnapped to my list of challenges accepted. Although"—she shot him a look—"they weren't really offered, more thrust on me. Where are we exactly?"

"Miles from the nearest road, nearest person. We're quite alone."

"Oh." She frowned.

"Another challenge… being alone."

"But I'm not. You're here."

He leaned forward and took the Go Pro camera from her and turned it off. He raised an eyebrow. "Anticipation is good for publicity. Let them wonder what you're up to, what you're doing. Your ratings will be even higher."

He let the boat glide into shore, pulled out a chilly bin and stepped with it onto the small beach. The sun was high overhead and bathed the canyon and small beach with its hot rays.

He turned, half-expecting her to have dived into the river and swum off. But she was right behind him. Seems the unexpected didn't faze her. She pulled the inflatable dinghy onto the small sandy beach.

"I can do that," said Max, turning to help.

"So can I," she said, pulling the boat in securely before standing, hands on hips, looking around her.

He resolutely tried to restrict his gaze to her eyes. "So it would appear. A woman of many talents."

"Oh, yes." She approached him. "I can look after myself."

She passed him by with a glance which told him in no uncertain terms that he wasn't to mess with her. Shame, because that's all he could think of doing.

"Drink?"

"Water if you have it? Or, let me guess, is it only Champagne in there? Chilling, I should imagine, in a bucket of ice."

He held the bottle up for her to see. "Sorry to disappoint you, I'm right out of Champagne." Her eyes widened with surprise. "No. I have hot dogs and beer."

Intrigued, she peered inside the chilly bin. "I don't see any hot dogs."

"Because they're not cooked yet."

He reached into the boat and withdrew a barbecue and set it up on a rock, and uncapped the beers, using each one as the opener for the other. He held one out to her. "There's some water in the chilly bin, if you prefer."

She took the beer. "So what's this all about, Max? Trying to surprise me?"

"Why would I bother with that?"

"Because I interest you. No doubt because I haven't fluttered my eyelashes and fallen into your bed."

"I see you're an expert on the male of the species."

She shrugged. "People always want things they can't have."

"You do realize there's only one way to test that hypothesis."

She shot him a look of mock annoyance. "I don't intend to make myself available simply to see if you're still interested, if that's what you mean."

He laughed. "Fair enough. But now you have me curious. What is it that interests Laura McKinney?"

She came up close to him, her eyes searching his face. Then she relaxed her expression and raised an eyebrow. "That hot dog you mentioned."

"Right." He laughed, lighting the BBQ, aware that it would take more than a kidnapping to get Laura to reveal that part of her she hid from everyone, which intrigued him more than anything else. A beautiful girl was simply that. But a beautiful girl who was full of contradictions and mystery was something else entirely—a physical, emotional and intellectual puzzle to unravel. Something which definitely piqued his interest. "Hot dog coming up."

HOT DOGS CONSUMED, she took a swig of beer and leaned back on the rocks and closed her eyes. "Ah, this is nice."

It certainly was, he couldn't help thinking.

She opened her eyes suddenly with a frown. "Do you think they'll be worrying about me?"

"No. I told Chelsey what I was doing, and she was going to let Kelly know."

"Ah, all part of the plan, then."

"Yes, as is this." Max picked up the GoPro and aimed it at her. "Something for the fans when we get back." She didn't fiddle with her hair or looks, but continued to look at him, a slow smile on her face. "Say hello."

He turned it on and nodded at her. Like the professional she was, she spoke straight to camera, describing how she'd been whisked away by someone tall, dark and handsome, for lunch in a deserted spot on the river. She looked up at Max and winked.

That wink. It was all it took for him to deviate from the plan and want to show her something unexpected. He fumbled with the button on the Go-Pro, set it down on a rock, and came over to her. "Well, Laura."

"Well, Max."

She licked her lips and she reached out for him, grabbing his hand. "Come here," she murmured.

He didn't need asking twice. He placed his free hand firmly on the rocks beside her, bracing himself away from her, not trusting himself to touch her body anywhere other than her lips. It was Laura who pulled his face to hers, his mouth to hers.

His senses were bombarded with stimuli: the taste of her, the sweet smell of her and the feel of her soft lips—more vulnerable than he'd imagined and far more arousing.

With the rushing of the water competing with the surge of his blood through his veins, the kiss deepened.

Her breath hitched as his tongue touched hers and for one long moment their tongues caressed and all he could think about was hot sex—as hot as the sun which blazed down on them.

He'd never experienced a kiss like it before. As well as sensuality, what surprised him was that there was a kind of refreshing innocence there, too. It was in the way she held his hand between them and kept her body slightly apart, slightly stiff, as if holding back. And yet the kiss was her—stripped bare.

It was Max who pulled away first. He still held her hand, and with the other, brushed away a strand of still wet hair from her face. "You're a very surprising woman."

Her eyes lingered on his lips. "That's what they tell me."

"They? All the people you kiss?"

"Like most men you've confused adventure with promiscuity. I don't go around kissing people."

That made sense. It explained the rawness and unsophistication of the kiss, and the complete and utter sensuality of it. "Then I feel honored."

"No, you don't. No need to say stupid things like that to me."

She stepped away and looked around at the scenery. Like the kiss, it was raw, passionate, the water of the river surging past, sending spray bouncing off the rocks, as it channeled through the narrow pass. He watched her pace across to the water's edge.

"Even if it's true?"

She glanced at him. "*Especially* if it's true." She returned her gaze out to the river and up to the slender stretch of blue sky, just as the sun dipped behind the cliffs. She shivered. "There's something about this place. Something more challenging than…" She trailed off but he knew it wasn't so much the place that had challenged her, but the kiss. He knew because he felt the same.

He handed her some thermals he'd brought with him.

"Best cover up now the sun's gone. It can get cold. We'll get on our way. I'll deliver you back to your adoring public."

"Right," she said, but there was a trace of reluctance, sadness almost, in her voice which made him pause as he gathered the things and look at her.

With her slender, tanned bikini-clad figure, sun-bleached hair which hung in messy tresses down her back, she was a goddess of nature, but he sensed there was an unease under the skin of this goddess which wasn't often exposed. It intrigued him.

He tossed the rest of the things into his bag, remembering the GoPro at the last minute, and placed them in the boat. She waded carefully through the water, got into the boat and pulled on the fleece.

He unlooped the rope from the rock and jumped in.

"Ready?"

"Yes."

"You okay?"

"It's just the post-thrill setting in. You know, after an hour or so the adrenaline wears off."

"Maybe I should give you some more, then." He tossed her a life jacket. "Better put this on."

He started the engine and steered them out into the middle of the river.

She grinned and the public face of Laura was back again. "Why?" she shouted above the noise of the water.

The water became noisier the further into the middle they went. It swirled dangerously around rocks between which a thin channel ran, the water fast and smooth as it rushed toward what appeared to be a sheer cliff face.

Her eyes widened with fear. "Where's the river gone?" she shrieked.

"Through that cave. You didn't think I *wasn't* going to give you a thrill to remember, did you? You'd better hold on tight. And keep your head down."

He focused on steering the boat through the twists and turns, revving back when required, before shooting through the black tunnel, the roof of which came perilously close to their heads.

They flew out the other side, skimming the water, and were momentarily held in the place between air and water, mist all around, emerging from it with a splash as they bounced once more onto the water of the swiftly flowing river.

Shouts from the river bank rang out and Laura looked around and waved at the crowds who'd gathered to watch Laura McKinney take on the famed Dog Leg rapid.

"How did they know?" Laura asked.

"I may have mentioned it to a few people."

She laughed. "That was amazing! Can we do it again?"

"I'm at your command. Just tell me when." With that, he steered the boat to the shore. He handed her her bag and she was swallowed up by adoring crowds.

His mate who'd loaned him the boat helped him haul it to shore. "You were longer than we thought."

"Got caught up."

"Huh. Don't let any of her fans know, there's a queue a mile long to get close to that one."

They both glanced at Laura who was talking ten to the dozen, interacting with her fans in front of a camera held by one of her team.

"I'm not surprised. She's pretty special."

His friend raised an eyebrow. "Max Connelly! Don't tell me you've fallen under her spell."

Max shook his head. He hadn't fallen under the spell Laura cast on her fans. But he was sure intrigued by the contradiction that was at the heart of the woman. So public, so natural, and yet… there was a part of her that was hidden, for all the exposure; a part of her, he suspected, which was afraid. But of what? He had no idea but he reckoned it would be more than a little interesting finding out.

LAURA CLIMBED into the back of the Land Rover and tossed the GoPro into Kelly's hands. "There's the footage from the jump and also some of me having lunch on the shore."

Kelly caught it and popped it into her pocket. "I'll check it through and then upload it as soon as we get back to the lodge."

"Kelly! No checking. I want the real me to come through, not some edited version. Okay?"

Kelly shook her head and sighed. "You're crazy, Laura. What if your boobs fell out during the fall."

"It wouldn't be the first time."

"What if your nose was running when you emerged from the water?"

"Wouldn't worry me."

"Okay, okay. Just as it is."

"I've nothing to hide. I want it all out there."

"Sure thing, Laura."

IT WASN'T until an hour later that Max emerged from his meeting with Chelsey and was able to retreat to his man-cave.

The first thing he did was turn on YouTube to Laura's channel. Seems he couldn't get enough of her, just like millions of others around the world. But there was no recent upload.

He kept it on while he went into the wet room and took a quick shower. Then he heard a roar from the TV and he recognized it for the bungy jump. He wrapped a towel around his waist and walked into the office, watching the big screen which was filled with shots taken from Laura's GoPro of the rapid descent and the plunge into the river. It looked amazing. As did Laura herself after she'd gotten into the boat and turned the camera on herself and finished up the piece. The camera went blank and Max waited for the footage he took on the shore. Maybe it didn't film for some reason. Then it came on, Laura glistening in the sunlight talking about her solo lunch.

Max grinned and was about to turn the TV off at the end of the clip except... it didn't end. The camera shifted as he placed it high up on a rock and went to turn it off. But it continued to film.

Max watched aghast as he came into view, a very close up view, and Laura's arms snaked around his naked back and drew him close to her and their lips met. The camera caught nothing of Laura's caution, only the entirely sensuous, lustful nature of the kiss. It must have been something to do with the angle of the camera. Their faces filled the screen. You saw nothing of the distance of their bodies, nothing of the fact that both were clothed—Laura's hair covered the thin white straps of her bikini and for all the world it looked like two naked people, kissing, a prelude to intense love-making.

Max sat down on the couch as if he'd been pushed. Except they hadn't been making love. Except he knew Laura wouldn't have wanted to get this naked in public view. She'd really been caught out this time. And she'd think it was his fault—that he'd done it on purpose.

3

"THAT KISS!!! IS LAURA SIMPLY BEING FRIENDLY, OR IS THERE MORE TO IT?" @TELLTALEGIRL #SMOOCHIES

*L*aura sat astride the chair, resting her chin on its back as she watched the kiss one more time.

"Jesus, Laura! You don't hang about, do you?" Kelly said, freezing the frame on the kiss.

Like most filming, it showed only one side of things—one aspect of the experience. In this case, it showed none of the chasteness, and all of the passion and electricity. Her stomach tightened with desire at the memory of Max's lips pressed against hers, of the way he'd slid his tongue along her lips and she'd opened her mouth to him. A shiver of desire snaked down her spine.

"Man, it's hot in here." Laura pushed up the old-fashioned sash window and leaned outside. A glint of light on the hill alerted her to the fact that a camera was trained on her. Let it, it didn't worry her, unlike the intimate image on the screen. She turned around to look at it again.

"I'm not surprised you're hot. *I'm* hot. Anyone looking at that image will be hot. And your life has just got a whole lot hotter."

Laura shrugged and crossed her arms. "Thought that was what you and Chelsey wanted."

"I guess. But we hadn't planned on something like this. Telltale Girl has already commented on it on her blog. What on earth got into you?"

"I'd have thought that was obvious. If I'm hot now, he's even hotter. Just look at him."

"You're surrounded by hot men. But you don't jump them all."

"I don't 'jump' any of them." She walked closer to the screen, picked up the remote control and pressed play once more. The kiss finished, they parted and Max was seen clearly. "I just went with the flow. Like I always do."

"You've never gone this far before." Kelly rose and poured them both coffees. She looked out across the hills, now bathed in early morning sunlight. "There's something about this place. You've been different here."

Laura grunted. "I'm no different here than anywhere else!" She accepted a coffee from Kelly who raised an eyebrow.

"Really?"

"Yes, really," said Laura, taking a sip of her coffee. "It's beautiful and all that… and those mountains." She gestured to the ice-capped ridge of the Remarkables. "They're something else." She narrowed her eyes in thought. "Kind of inspiring."

"Inspiring enough to seduce a man… or *be* seduced by a man?"

She glared at Kelly. "I'm into flirtation, not seduction. That's not my style."

"It might not be your style, but I'd say that Max Connelly has the whole seduction thing going on."

"That'll be useful, then, won't it, for whatever you and Chelsey have planned for us."

"That kiss will take things a whole lot further than we'd planned. It could work. Although I still can't believe you filmed it."

"I didn't. *He* did."

Laura would have laughed at Kelly's shocked expression if she hadn't been so shocked herself. She embraced all challenges but they were always on her terms, her decision. But this time? Max had stolen the initiative and she wasn't sure how she felt about it.

Her initial feelings of anger and betrayal, at having been tricked, had swiftly given way to respect. He'd played her at her own game and won. It triggered her already well-honed competitive instinct.

Kelly strode across the room and picked up the phone. "That's not on! I'll ring Chelsey."

"Why not talk to her? She's only down the corridor."

"Some things"—Kelly emphasized her words with a shake of the phone—"are best done in a business-like way, from a distance." She turned away from Laura. "Chelsey? What's going on? This wasn't what we agreed!"

Laura sighed, scrolling down the Twitter feed on her own phone. There was silence as Kelly listened. A few perfunctory replies followed and Kelly finished the call.

"Seems she was out of the loop, too. Max pulled this one by himself."

"I don't know what you're worried about, it'll be good for us both in the long run. That was what you wanted, wasn't it?"

"Hm. You could be right." Kelly began to pace back and forward. "It's something new for you, something that could stir up wider interest. Yeah, actually this could work."

For all of Laura's words of reassurance to Kelly, Laura still felt unsettled by Max's stunt. Laura swung between admiration that he'd bested her, indignation for the same reason, but above all, intrigue. She was intrigued to see how far this would go before one or the other of them went too far.

That had been one hell of a kiss and he, it was turning out, was one hell of a man. Intrigued, definitely. Seduced? The jury was still out on that one.

"Hey look, people are wondering if this is a challenge!" Kelly continued to scroll through the comments and looked up with a grin. "Seems you're being challenged to date Max Connelly. You up for it?"

Laura didn't have to think twice. She stepped forward and typed in her usual response—a smiley face with a thumbs-up.

MAX HAD his staff circulating around the Lodge and grounds trying to find Laura. He'd only ventured out of his office once to be swarmed by people before he beat a hasty retreat. He tried her cellphone but it went straight to voicemail.

He looked out the window at his resort which was over-run with people now that Laura's latest video had gone viral. Seemed it was good for business. He turned away. He'd managed to create a video which had done precisely what Laura tried to do with all her videos. Then why did he feel so bad?

He'd thought he'd turned off the video. He didn't usually make such blunders but then, he had been about to get up close and personal with a beautiful woman and his mind hadn't been entirely focused on the camera.

He didn't even mind the footage from his own point of view—it was hardly damning, a kiss, maybe not entirely chaste, between two people. It had obviously brought him publicity which was always needed.

No, what he felt bad about was Laura. She was always

open and honest and she'd believe he hadn't been. It wasn't in his nature to trick people but she wasn't to know that. He had to see her, he had to explain.

He flicked on the computer screen and watched the comments come pouring in under her video. Broken hearts, both male and female, as well as cheers and encouragement. And, finally, asking her whether this was a new challenge.

There was a knock at the door and Chelsey entered, without waiting to be asked. She raised her eyebrows in a 'really?' expression and closed the door quietly behind her.

"Hey, Max. Are you sure you require my services? It looks like you're doing a pretty good job on your own."

He thrust his fingers through his hair and shook his head with a sigh. "Not intentionally, Chelsey, not intentionally."

"Albeit in an underhanded kind of way." She cocked her head to one side, challenging him to dispute the fact. She received a glare for her trouble. Chelsey walked over to the screen and picked up the remote, clicking the infra-red pointer to the comments section to highlight her point. "Who's the sexy man?" she read out. She glanced at him. "No reply to the media yet? It's not like you *not* to admit to being a sexy man."

He propped his elbows on the table with his forehead rested on fisted hands, and shook his head.

"Why, Max! It's almost as if you regret it." She glanced once more at the frozen image of Max and Laura mid-kiss. "And yet you look as if you were enjoying it." She clicked the zoom button on to Laura's closed eyes, and lips, where his tongue was just visible against her lips. There was only one word for her expression—orgasmic. "Huh, and Laura appears to be, too. Although with your tongue—"

Max reached out and hit a key on the computer and the image vanished. "Enough! Stop damn well teasing me,

Chelsey. You might be my ex, you might be my oldest employee—"

"Oldest?" she asked archly.

"But that doesn't give you the right to tease the hell out of me," Max continued, ignoring Chelsey's interruption.

"I beg to differ," she said, as she brushed down the old settee, tutting at its shabbiness. "If I don't, then who will?"

"How about my sisters and brothers for starters? Believe me, there will be a queue of people waiting to have a go at me."

"The more, the merrier. Anyway, despite what you think, I'm not here to annoy you." She turned the screen on again and scrolled down to the bottom comment. "*This* is what I'm here for."

He read out loud the final comment. "Is this a new challenge?" He looked at Chelsey accusingly. "You want me and Laura to turn this into some kind of publicity stunt? You're mad."

"I'm your marketing manager which, true, probably does make me mad by definition. But you only need to glance out the window to see what the publicity is doing for you already."

Max didn't need to glance. He could hear the hubbub outside; he could hear people calling Laura's name, and the roar of TV vans climbing up the hill to the Lodge.

She laughed and flung her arms out wide. "Max! It's the opportunity of a lifetime. You don't have to seek out any additional publicity, you don't have to organize anything. Just you and Laura. The two of you combined are dynamite. And *will* be dynamite for the business."

"It's not right. It's personal, not public. And, besides, Laura would never go for it."

"Is that right?"

Chelsey turned the computer to Laura's blog, posted half

an hour earlier. He quickly read it and felt deflated. She'd gone on record as accepting the challenge without even talking to him about it. Seemed she had no qualms about making the personal public. Maybe because it wasn't personal to her. Why the hell was he fretting about having stuffed up? This was Laura, he reminded himself, and he'd entered new territory with her.

He knew how to avoid women who had marriage on their minds, and he knew how to escape from women who'd slipped through his first defenses but who'd then turned into master manipulators. But Laura? She didn't fall into any mold. And he was all the more intrigued because of it.

"Sure, why not? So what's your plan?"

Chelsey grinned. "One." She counted with one finger. "You and Laura become an item." She gestured toward the screen. "Seems she's happy with that. Two." She counted a second finger. "Play it up for all it's worth. And it will be worth some, I can assure you. I've had approaches from all around the world for interviews and the inside gossip on you and your relationship with Laura. And three." She counted on her third finger. "Have fun. Because it won't be convincing if you don't."

"Is that all?" asked Max wryly. "Go out with a sexy girl, talk it up, have fun and, oh yes, I mustn't forget, do it all under the glare of the world's media. Sounds wonderful."

Grinning, Chelsey approached him, and ran her finger down his collar and turned it out. "Max, who are you kidding? You're talking to me, remember. You'll love it."

"Okay." He looked down at her. He could never deny her when she turned those puppy dog eyes on him. "I'll talk to her, see if we can do something."

"Looks like she's decided to do something, with or without your agreement. She must be pretty sure of you." Chelsey winked and left the room.

Max buttoned up his shirt in front of the mirror, pushed his fingers through his short hair and stared at himself. What the hell was he doing? But, while part of him was not comfortable with the idea, a much larger, more influential part of him most definitely was. His intense attraction to Laura overruled any doubts. She was gorgeous, fun, and there was that part of her she hid from the public, which he'd yet to figure out. And, they'd both make a fortune by hanging out together for a week. What was not to like?

HE DIDN'T NEED to phone her to find out where she was. He followed the sounds of the crowds. He, too, was soon stopped by journalists and bloggers, wanting to know if it was true.

He refrained from asking "what was true?", simply smiling in a way which he hoped was amenable and mysterious at the same time, and carried on through the gardens of the Lodge to where he'd spotted Laura.

Her blonde hair drew him like a beacon, lighting up the already bright, sunlit garden. She was in perpetual motion, walking around talking to everyone, answering questions, inclining her head toward children. Not for the first time, he wondered what drove her. He hesitated, wanting to watch her from afar for a few moments, but he'd forgotten the people who were following him, and who now jostled him from behind. He sighed with irritation. Seemed there was a downside to fame after all.

Laura looked up suddenly. "Max!" she shouted and the crowd parted, curiosity on their faces, as he faced Laura, who wore cowboy boots, the usual torn jeans, skimpy lace camisole and a weathered Stetson on her head. Her voice was firm, her smile wide but her eyes had a hint of something else behind them. Something steely and dangerous.

"Laura!" He paused. "Darling!" he added for good measure. He wasn't going to let her take the lead here. She might have accepted the challenge and proclaimed their relationship before he'd had a chance to ask her out, but he'd be damned if he'd be portrayed to the world as some meek beta guy.

"Max!" She reached out for him but he caught her hand in his and twisted it up to his lips and kissed it. Surprise flashed across her face but she quickly recovered.

"Laura!" He pulled her to him and kept hold of her hand firmly. She tried to tug it away but he refused to let it out of his grip. Her smile froze a little.

"Are we going to keep on calling each other's names?" she asked.

"Laura!" He grinned. "Why not? It gives a kind of apt stage quality to it all, don't you think?"

"I guess it makes it easier than actually talking."

He inclined his head so he could be heard by her alone. "Sorry, I didn't realize you wanted to talk as well as date. I hadn't read *that* online."

She smiled cockily and pulled away. "You gotta keep up, Max." She turned and smiled at a teenager who excitedly asked for a photo of Laura with her. The photo taken, the teenager ran off shrieking to find her friends.

He offered his arm. "Care for a stroll, Laura?"

"Why not?" She slipped her arm through his and walked along the path, an unnerving experience when being followed by hordes of strangers, jostling to get close to them. "How can you stand this?" he whispered, his head bowed to hers.

"It's my life. It's what I choose to do."

He shook his head. "It's crazy-making stuff."

She stopped and smiled but the smile didn't reach her eyes which were icy. She raised an eyebrow. "And so is being videoed when I think I'm on private time. Seems you forgot to tell me you'd left the camera running," she said from between gritted teeth.

"I didn't know I had, darlin'" he said. "Believe it or not." He glanced at the crowds who were closing in and tugged her arm. "Let's keep moving, shall we? Before the pack descends."

She shrugged. "Sure, why not? It's a nice day," she said as if the sunny afternoon was the only reason she agreed.

As they continued along the path he glanced at her but she looked away, the jut of her jaw telling him all he needed to know about her mood.

"I'm surprised you're angry, given the fact that you live your life in full view of the world." Still no response. "Surely it's business as usual for you?"

"What I do," she said carefully, "I'm in control of. I don't like these kind of surprises."

They stopped at a viewing platform and looked out.

"Believe it or not, I'm not exactly thrilled either."

"Really?" she said coolly. "I hear that the publicity has already brought in a load of business enquiries for the Lodge. And you're trying to tell me that that wasn't planned?"

Max leaned against the railing, narrowing his eyes at the bright expansive view. "We don't know each other well, Laura, so you can believe me or not. That's your prerogative. I'm ambitious for my businesses and I drive a hard bargain. But one thing I don't do is succeed by tricking people. That's not on. If I'd wanted to take a video of us kissing I'd have told you. But I didn't. Okay?" He didn't want to wait for an answer. He looked around. "Shall we get going?"

She placed a hand on his arm and for the first time since they'd stopped walking, he got her to look at him. "For real? You didn't film on purpose?"

"No, Laura, I didn't. I'm not in the habit of getting what I

43

want by underhand means. I have many faults, but that's not one of them."

A slow smile spread over her face. "Apart from kidnapping me mid-river."

He shrugged. "Apart from that, of course."

"Okay," she said, continuing to walk. "I believe you. But don't do it again, otherwise I'll tell the world what a terrible kisser you are." She raised an eyebrow and grinned.

He stopped in mid stride. "They'd never believe you. I'd bring evidence forward to the contrary."

"Don't care. Millions of people would believe *me*."

He pressed his hand to his chest as if he'd been stabbed. "*You* are a cruel woman."

"Not if you do as I say."

"You're also a controlling woman."

"I'm a grown woman, that's all. Maybe you're not used to being with grown women."

"Oh, I can tell you right now, I am. They're the only kind I like."

Did he imagine it, or did her smile falter slightly? Before he could call her on it, she'd recovered, apparently into full organizational mode.

"Right. Now, Kelly thinks we should make more of this, seeing how well it's going. I've had approaches from big companies for product endorsement."

He shook his head in disbelief. "You'd really pretend to have a relationship with me, for some product endorsements?"

"Pretend is the operative word. And the endorsements total a million."

"Hm." He glanced around to see the crowd was edging nearer. He continued walking and she fell into step. "And Chelsey is impressed with the interest we've had from around the world. It could set my lodge on the map, make it the kind of place I've always wanted to turn it into."

"Then how about it?"

He felt as if he were being pushed into something. He wasn't in the habit of being pushed, rather, of leading. He pulled her toward him and bent his mouth to her ear so only she could hear. "You're full of surprises."

She smiled and looked around at the people who jostled and swarmed around them. "Max says I'm full of surprises!" Everyone laughed and Max smiled through gritted teeth.

She tried to move her hand out of his grip but he allowed his smile to broaden and he held her even more firmly. "And you're not the only one," he said to all and sundry. "I have a surprise for you."

She looked a little uncertain but covered it quickly by a flashing smile. "And what's that?"

"No, that's the first rule of surprises—don't reveal them until the last moment, or else—"

"They cease to be surprises?"

"Exactly. So come with me, Ms. McKinney."

It had done the trick, set her off-guard, given him the upper hand, even if it meant he had to think quickly to work out exactly what the surprise was going to be. Seems he was as competitive as she was.

In a vain attempt to disperse the crowd of onlookers who were intent on following them, he steered her firmly toward a walkway. It led to a viewing point overlooking the whole of the valley with Queenstown nestled beside the long blue length of Lake Wakatipu.

Despite his choice of destination, people were determined to watch them, clambering dangerously on the sides of the rocks surrounding the lookout, projecting boom micro-phones over their heads to catch their every word. Nearby the sound of a chopper grew louder until it swept around in front of them, photographers snapping as they went. The chopper circled around once more, to make another sweep.

Laura smiled. "So what's your surprise?"

"A challenge, Laura, what else?"

Only he could have seen her smile falter a little.

"I only take challenges via the 'net."

"Oh, my challenge will be on the Internet in seconds. You can consider it at your leisure after you've seen it on your phone, if you prefer." His mind was still whirring with bizarre possibilities, not yet having settled on one.

She grinned. "You haven't got one, have you? You're making this up as you go along, trying to beat me at my own game." She threw her head back and laughed. "Okay. Whatever you come up with, I accept."

But he didn't laugh. Suddenly he decided to go along with the most extreme challenge that had popped into his mind, been rejected, but had refused to leave. He thought about the ring of his mother's he wore around his neck.

"Go on, then," she teased.

It broke down the last vestige of sanity in his mind. He gestured toward the crowds. "Hey, everyone! She's accepted my challenge!"

Laura's frown at being pre-empted was quickly replaced by a wide smile. "You know me!" she shouted to the crowds.

"What's the challenge this time, Laura?" someone shouted.

She smiled. "Max? Maybe you'd like to tell them?"

"Sure, Laura." He put his arm around her and hugged her. Her body stiffened under his embrace, at the same time as her smile widened. She might be taking the lead on this, but he was determined to push her out of her comfort zone. "Laura's agreed to a question I haven't asked her yet, haven't you, darling?"

He'd have laughed at her reaction if he wasn't himself stunned by his own behavior.

The crowd hollered, feeling the blood was up. He let go of her hand. She wasn't going anywhere now. He unclipped the chain from around his neck and slid off the ring.

Her face flickered between frowning and smiling. He'd really unsettled her which made him more certain to go ahead. He'd out-maneuvered her and he felt the thrill of the win, quashing any remaining doubt. He took hold of her hand once more and got down on his knees, just as the chopper circled around again to a blast of flashes and shutter sounds.

"Laura McKinney, will you marry me?" He held out his mother's ring, the diamond flashing in the sunlight.

She looked down at him, her eyes bright with the light of a challenge accepted. She couldn't resist it and he knew it. No matter what other thoughts were spinning around her head. She'd always rise to the challenge, no matter how preposterous.

"Yes, Max Connelly, I will."

He didn't know who was more stunned, him or her. But, stunned or not, he rose, pushed his mother's ring on her finger and kissed her.

4

"MARRIAGE? NAH! UNLESS... IT'S FOR AT
LEAST SIX MONTHS—NOW THAT WOULD
BE A CHALLENGE!" @TELLTALEGIRL
#LAURASGETTINGMARRIED

*L*aura held the ring up to the cameras which were all focused on her hand. She twisted it this way and that, enjoying the flash of light against the plain gold, and wondering what the hell she'd just done.

It was one thing accepting challenges which called for her to eat something gross, or to risk life and limb in a feat of athleticism, but marriage? Her mind was numb, unable to grasp the full implications. But her gut knew what was going on—it twisted into a sickening clench. And the more it twisted, the wider her smile grew to cover it.

She was acutely aware of Max holding her hand tightly, as if he, too, could hardly believe what had just happened. Truth was, he probably couldn't. Max also had zero interest in marriage. It was a stunt. That's all it was. They'd marry and then divorce. Easy. It wouldn't mean anything to either of them.

"Laura! How does it feel to be engaged to be married?"

Married?! Just hearing that word, which she'd never thought of in relation to herself, made her stomach clench more tightly still. What the hell were they doing?

"Surreal!" Everyone laughed, but she couldn't. It was as if she'd stepped into a parallel universe. Everything looked the same, but everything was different.

"And Max? What made you pop the question?"

Max's grip on her hand tightened.

"I couldn't resist!" Max responded.

Laura knew it wasn't her he couldn't resist. She knew, because she was exactly the same. Just like her, Max was prey to his competitive instinct, and couldn't resist a challenge. And he was as stunned as she was with where it had led him.

The questions kept on coming.

"Laura! Is this love?"

She laughed uncomfortably. "That's for another challenge."

"If it's not love, then how long do you see your marriage lasting?"

Max interrupted. "If we could see into the future we'd tell you!"

There was laughter but the reporter didn't let it go. "It's got to be at least six months. Otherwise it wouldn't be a real challenge. That's what Telltale Girl is saying."

Laura and Max exchanged looks. His expression was a mirror of hers—fixed smile below shell-shocked eyes. She was right. His proposal challenge had been a knee-jerk reaction. That knowledge gave her strength. She turned back to the reporter. "Of course it's going to be at least six months. Isn't it, Max?"

"Of course," he repeated. He turned to the crowd. "Now, if you'll excuse us, we've a wedding to organize."

He pulled her away from the clamor of the world's press down a winding path.

"Hey! Where are we going?"

"Some place away from that lot," he said under his breath.

He opened a gate and locked it firmly behind them. Laura

waved to those who had followed them as far as they could. "See you later!"

They walked across a small lawn and into a rear entrance of the Lodge. Inside, she looked around. She'd never been in this part of the building before.

"Where are we?"

"My private quarters. I thought it was probably the only place where we could get away from that circus who follow you everywhere. How you cope with this all the time is beyond me."

"Well, Fiancée, you'd better learn quickly because you're going to be part of this 'circus' for at least six months."

Whatever he was going to say remained unsaid by the approach of Kelly and Chelsey, both with phones in hands, obviously having watched the whole thing online.

"Max!" said Chelsey.

"Laura!" said Kelly.

Laura and Max looked at each other briefly before they were swept off by their respective staff.

MAX HELD open the door for Chelsey and she strode into the room, her stiletto heels stabbing the stone-slabbed floor. He couldn't help thinking that they'd be the last thing Laura would ever wear. He'd only seen her in Doc Marten boots or barefoot. Usually barefoot.

He turned on the screen and flicked channels to see himself proposing to Laura. Was his life always going to be like this? When he wasn't with the woman who constantly preyed on his mind, among other things, he'd watch her on the big screen? Seems he'd caught the madness of Laura, like everyone else.

Chelsey turned and glared at him. "What the hell made you say that, Max? Marriage? Are you out of your mind?"

He shrugged. He wasn't in the habit of agreeing with his marketing manager, but he couldn't contradict her, so he remained silent.

She huffed, shook her head and glanced at the screen again. "And she's as mad as you. Why the hell did she agree to marry you?"

He shrugged again but she pinned him with her eyes—it was obviously one shrug too many. "Because I'm a catch?" he offered helpfully.

"No you're not! You're a workaholic, macho oaf, who's so out of touch with his feelings that he considers pig hunting in sub zero temperatures to be a good date."

"How many times do I have to apologize for that," he grumbled, picking up the remote control to turn off the computer.

"Don't turn it off!" snapped Chelsey.

He turned it off. "If you're done shouting, go! I've work to do."

"Correction. We have work to do. I'm not going anywhere."

He rolled his eyes. "What the hell did I do to deserve you?"

"Nothing. You just got lucky."

She opened one of the cupboards which lined the wall, found a jumble of sports equipment and closed it again with a grunt before opening another one.

"Which of these damn cupboard do you keep your coffee machine in?" Before he could respond she'd discovered what she was looking for and flicked it on. Then she turned, folded her arms across her chest and fixed her gaze on him.

"First up. Tell me how it happened."

Max leaned back against the wall, and shrugged. "How do these things normally happen?" He was playing for time and she knew it.

"Well, Max, people date, they fall in love and decide they want to live the rest of their lives together. That's how it's normally done. And given you've only known Laura a few days, I think we can rule 'normal' out, don't you?"

"Truth is, Chelsey, I don't know how it happened. One minute she was needling me about something, the next I found I'd raised the stakes a notch. Then she came back with something, and then I found myself saying stuff…" He trailed off. He really didn't want to say out loud what he'd said only moments earlier.

"'Will you marry me', kind of stuff?"

"Yeah." He paced across the room. "I guess I wanted to give her a real challenge, something unpredictable."

"Something so unpredictable, *you* didn't even see it coming."

He shot her a glance. Sometimes it was annoying working with someone who knew you so well.

"So, let me get this straight," Chelsey continued. "You began by hi-jacking her bungy jump to have a little alone time with her during which you filmed your kiss."

"That was an accident."

"And she believes that?"

He shrugged. "She seemed to. I haven't had much of a chance to talk to her."

"And yet you've had a chance to propose marriage to her."

"That was different." Chelsey's interrogation was beginning to get on his nerves. He was the boss around here. How come he always got himself surrounded by stroppy women?

"Go on. Tell me how it happened."

"Why do you need to know in detail?"

"Because I want to put myself in Laura's shoes, try to get into her head, see what it is that made her accept. Understanding something is half the battle."

"I didn't know this was a battle."

"Of course it is, Max! It's business. And business is war. Don't you read your Chinese literature?"

"Not recently."

"And it's a war that we need to make sure we win."

"Chelsey! What the hell has gotten into you?"

There was a silence between them and Chelsey's expression changed. There was something in her eyes, a hurt, that he'd not seen in a long time. But before he could place it, she turned away and busied herself with making the coffee. "Just tell me why you proposed," she said in a quieter tone. The fight had slipped out of her. "Give me something to work with."

He shrugged again. How could he explain the inexplicable? "I couldn't help myself. She kept saying one thing, and I couldn't help taking it one step beyond. Then she'd take it a step beyond that and—"

"The rest is history." She sighed.

He grunted. "A short one, I hope. I don't want to be married, just like I don't want to participate in any other disaster."

"You know, Max, not everyone would consider it a disaster to get married to the internet's most eligible bachelorette."

"Then they're more insane than me."

"Impossible," Chelsey muttered. She looked at the old sofa with distaste before sitting down gingerly and turning the computer screen back on.

While Chelsey scrolled through the comments which were pouring in on Laura's YouTube channel, Twitter, Instagram pictures and all the other social media which she dominated, Max looked through the window at the bright blue skies, rugged mountains and sweeping golden tussock that rolled on seemingly forever.

He loved that damned view. He felt it in his veins, it was

the home of his grandparents and their parents before them. And it was the place his mother had adored, maybe even more than the gentle shores of Belendroit, and it was here that he could remember her, could keep her memory alive, make her proud. If this marriage helped him do that, surely that was reason enough for it?

He looked up. Chelsey's expression had changed. He groaned. "What is it?"

"Merely"—she looked up at the ceiling, as her fingers tapped on the threadbare arm of the sofa—"thinking of ways we can capitalize on this madness of yours." She jumped up, pulled out a drawer below the computer, and had a quick rummage. "Don't you keep anything useful in here? iPad, tablet, pen, paper?"

"No."

"Then let's go to my office and turn this thing around."

OKAY, the women in his life—Chelsey, sisters and friends—might be a stroppy lot, but sometimes it was good being surrounded by them, Max thought as he put his feet up on the desk and watched Chelsey and her assistant fill out the rough plan she and Max had come up with.

He could never understand men who belittled women, who couldn't appreciate the sheer brilliance of women's minds. Men dismissed women for their lack of logic, but it was women's ability to blend the logical with the illogical which always floored Max with its utter brilliance.

Like this. He'd called it a disaster. Chelsey had called it madness and had come up with a plan which had turned the madness into something which had a passing resemblance to sanity.

Yep, those leaps of imagination or intuition, call it what you will, which took a mundane idea and transformed it into another thing entirely, based on nothing like the rational logic which he'd built his life on, had him constantly in awe of women. Given the choice, he'd work with women any time.

But he couldn't replace his mates when it came to relaxing. Drinking beer, hunting, fishing, all things he liked to do. Women's crazy minds might be awe-inspiring but they weren't relaxing. You knew where you were when you were hanging out with your mates. The language was earthy, the behavior was predictable, and the activities were perfectly enjoyable mindless things in which they could flex their muscles and pit themselves against the elements. As the sister closest in age to him, Lizzi, frequently pointed out, Max and his friends hadn't evolved since caveman times. But what Lizzi didn't realize was how much simpler life was living by those rules. And he was all for a simple life.

He glanced around the room and rubbed his stubbly chin at the sight of Chelsey, phone clamped to ear, and her assistant, head to head, as they tweaked a spreadsheet. He sighed. His life had been reduced to a spreadsheet.

Chelsey ended the call and tossed the phone onto the desk. She leaned over the desk to Max. "Right, Max. I've cleared it with Laura's people. We're giving a press conference later on today."

"By we, I'm guessing you mean Laura and me."

"Correct. And I've arranged a meeting for the two of you right now. To get over the awkwardness."

"What awkwardness?"

"You didn't see that in Laura's eyes?" She shook her head. "Max Connelly, what am I going to do with you?"

"Treat me with respect, maybe?" he said, getting to his feet. "Treat me as your boss, perhaps? As someone who could fire you at any time?"

There was a moment's pause and then Chelsey and her

assistant exchanged glances and burst out laughing.

He grunted with annoyance and walked to the door where he turned and stabbed his finger at Chelsey. "Just as well you're adorable, Chelsey Jones, and good at your job, or else you'd be out of here."

But she didn't respond with her usual smart come-back, instead he glimpsed a naked hurt in her eyes which always nearly broke his heart. She hid it well, but he knew it was there and he felt guilty. Guilty that he couldn't love her as she loved him.

"Right, Max, whatever you say." She rolled her eyes, unconvincingly, at least to him. "Now, go and make peace with your fiancée so we can give a convincing show later."

He grinned. "I love the way you say 'we'. It's like I won't be alone in this marriage fiasco."

Chelsey glared at him. "Of course you're not alone. You'll have Laura." A wicked grin stole across her face, any vulnerability now completely gone, or at least hidden. "Till death us do part."

He suddenly felt less good-humored, less guilty, and thrust his hands in his pockets and walked over to the door.

FROM HER VANTAGE point by the window, Laura watched Max emerge from the front door and step into the sunshine. He walked looking straight ahead, apparently oblivious to the shouts of people trying to catch his attention and take his photograph. When a particularly obnoxious photographer stepped in front of him, Max didn't push him out the way like other men Laura had known, but simply looked at him, refusing to answer his questions. The man, for all his tenacity, stepped away, visibly shrinking under Max's laser-like glare.

Laura smiled. If she had to marry someone, Max was

more suitable than anyone else she'd ever met. At least he had the balls to stand up for himself—and her, when it came to it.

"Marriage? Really, Laura? Are you crazy?"

Laura sighed and turned back to face Kelly.

"You know I am."

"Max's marketing manager, Chelsey, has been in touch. She reckons we can do something with this. Something which will benefit the both of us."

"Benefit us?"

"It's a challenge for you—just like any other. If, as you say, you've no romantic interest in this guy, then that shouldn't be hard, should it?" Kelly paused and looked at Laura intently. "That is right, isn't it? You don't have any feelings for him?"

Laura dismissed the idea with a vague wave of her hand. "You know me. I like men, I like having them around, I adore flirting with them, but that's as far as it goes. I don't want anyone to own me and tell me what I can and can't do. I don't want to be tied to only one man."

"Then why, may I ask, are you marrying one?"

"Because, Kelly, as you say, it's a challenge. Like any other."

There was a knock at the door. "Hold that thought." Kelly rose to answer it. "A challenge, remember. And we'll deal with it like one. But this is a real living challenge, and you need to keep your eye on the ball on this one. Otherwise you might find it's your hardest challenge yet."

She opened the door to reveal Max Connelly, looking slightly less contained than usual.

Laura jumped up from the sofa and strode over to the door. "Well, if it isn't my fiancé." She held out the ring. "Thanks for the ring, by the way."

"I'll replace it with another one when I've a chance."

She looked at the ring, feeling unaccountably disappointed. Of all the elements of this afternoon's silliness, the ring had been the clear winner. It was beautiful, in an old-fashioned kind of way.

"You regret it already?"

"It's not that. The ring wasn't mine to give."

She shrugged. "Then it's not mine to take. You'd better have it back." She tried to pull it off her finger but it was stuck. "Sorry. I'll get some butter or something on to it. I don't usually wear rings. Kelly! How do you get a ring off that's stuck?"

Kelly glanced at her, with a glint in her eye. "You don't. You have to keep on wearing it."

Laura grinned but saw Max wasn't. "She's kidding. I'll get it off somehow. Anyway, how come you were walking around with a ring around your neck? Just being prepared, like a good Boy Scout?"

"It was my mother's. She died six years ago. We were always close. She gave me the ring on her death bed. She said it belongs to the woman I love and want to share my life with."

"Oh." Laura exhaled, stunned at the sudden revelation. It revealed a depth of emotion that was shocking after all the superficiality of the day. She hadn't really given Max's family, or his past, much thought. Everything had happened so fast. Max hadn't changed his expression and he'd spoken in a matter of fact way which she recognized. Because wasn't that how she dealt with her emotions—tucked them right away until she could almost believe she didn't have any? "Look, I'll get it to you as soon as I can. In the meantime, we'd better sort out what the hell we're going to do."

As if on cue, Chelsey entered the room. "Hello everyone! Hello engaged couple!" She and Kelly exchanged grins. "Let's sit down and work out how we're going to handle you guys."

"The hottest couple in New Zealand," Kelly couldn't resist adding.

Max sat. "Let's get on with it then. If there's one thing I hate, it's unfinished business."

Laura had to agree with him there.

BY THE END OF AN HOUR, they'd formulated a plan. They'd stick together for six months—long enough to satisfy Telltale Girl and all the other fans that this really was a challenge, and long enough to pull in some good contracts. The contracts would give Laura breathing space and Max some great publicity including holding international events at the Lodge next year. Then the marriage would be annulled and they'd go their separate ways.

It all made sense, Max thought to himself, until he caught a glimpse of his mother's ring on Laura's finger. The thought of what his mother would have made of this situation made him uncomfortable… and sad. His mother wouldn't have approved of what he was doing. She'd taken marriage and family very seriously. Her husband and her children had been her life. What would she have made of what he was doing? Max couldn't bear imagining what her reaction would have been like.

Laura had tried to slip off the ring a couple of times, but it still refused to budge and her finger was red and puffy with all the pulling.

"Don't worry, Laura," said Chelsey.

"I don't understand," said Laura with a frown holding up her hands. "My fingers look puffier than normal."

"Ah," dismissed Kelly, "probably the time of month."

Max suddenly felt uncomfortable.

"We can sort the ring out later," said Chelsey. "Leave it for now. We've enough things to organize. Like a wedding, eh, Kelly?"

"A beautiful white wedding," said Kelly.

Max's heart sunk further. "I'll leave you lot to it, then." He walked toward the door.

"You can't shake me off so easily, Max," said Chelsey. "I'm coming with you. There's things we need to discuss."

Max groaned. The sooner these six months were over, the better.

LAURA AND KELLY listened to Max and Chelsey's footfalls fade down the echoing walkway outside their room. Laura knew when they'd reached the public part of the Lodge by the shouts of welcome and questions with which they were bombarded.

Kelly let out a long low whistle. "He's something else. Think you've met your match there, Laura."

Laura shook her head. She refused to believe it.

"Are you sure you're okay with all of this? I mean, you'll be on your own with him, at night sometimes. Can you trust him to leave you alone?"

Laura moved to the window where she could see him and Chelsey engaging with the reporters. He was as macho as they came and yet... there was a quality about him which offset that. He was neither a bully, nor domineering. He had no need to be because he was strong in himself. He may take control of a situation—as he had, surprising her by picking her up from the bungy jump, surprising her with the marriage proposal—but, from what she'd seen of his interactions with Chelsey and his sisters, all strong women who patently adored him, he was totally respectful of women.

"Yes, I think I can trust him."

"What? Even when he left the camera rolling for the kiss?"

"He didn't mean to do that."

Kelly scoffed. "So he says."

"I could tell. I was there. He made no attempt to fiddle with the camera, to make sure it was focused on the right thing. Have you tried to use a GoPro without it being fixed onto anything? It's impossible. No, he put it on a ledge and forgot about it."

She sighed as she remembered what had happened next. It had been unexpected—of herself rather than him. No, she wasn't so much concerned about how Max would behave, but how she would.

Six months in which to behave herself with this man whose kisses stirred desires in her the like of which she'd never felt before. Six months. Could she do it? That would be the real challenge.

NIGHT HAD SETTLED ALL AROUND like a sheltering cloak. Apart from a lone car winding its way up the mountain road, and the rustle of the trees in the night breeze, there was no sound. And that was just how Max liked it.

He took a sip of his brandy and inhaled the cool mountain air. He was a night owl. He loved the end of the day when the work was done, when he was alone with his thoughts and this place which he loved so much.

If there was one place in the world where he felt at peace, this was it—with the mountains, the valley and lake far below, the wide skies littered with stars, and this place which his great-grandparents had built from nothing. Or it was, until he'd turned his life into a circus.

But not for long, he hurriedly reassured himself. It was a means to an end. And once that end had been achieved then the serene spirit which pervaded this place could settle and nurture, not just him, but all his visitors, for decades to come. A fitting legacy for his family, a fitting memorial to his mother.

Max frowned as the sound of the car penetrated his reverie. The car had turned off the main highway and was climbing the drive up to the Lodge. He glanced at his watch. Two in the morning? He walked around to the front of the building in time to see Laura jump out of the car, followed by Kelly.

Of course. Who else? He didn't think ten minutes had passed the whole evening when Laura hadn't come up in the conversation, despite her absence, as she fulfilled yet another engagement in Queenstown. And then there was her Twitter feed which sent tweets constantly pinging to his phone. And then, he had to admit, there were the in-between times when he'd escaped to his man-cave, turned on his computer and watched her. Seems he was becoming as obsessive about her as everyone else.

He stepped out of the shadows to greet them. "Had a good evening?"

Kelly jumped but Laura didn't turn a hair. Nerves of steel, Max thought.

"Yes, thanks. Queenstown was fun." Laura stepped toward him. She was wearing a short floral dress with the tiniest denim jacket over the top, its worn material and tears contrasting with the designer dress. On her feet were Doc Marten boots, their laces undone. "Your name came up a lot." She raised an eyebrow and smiled.

"Did they want to know where your fiancée was?" He smiled back. The whole thing seemed ludicrous away from the public gaze.

"Yeah, that and a million other things."

"Like what?"

She stepped closer, her eyes holding his gaze. "Wouldn't

you like to know." She reached out and pulled his hand which held his drink and smelled it while she looked up at him. That look. "Um. Smells delicious. What is it?"

"Cherry brandy." He cleared his throat because his voice had gone sexy-husky as he imagined other positions where she might be looking up at him from. "Not my usual drink. A new supplier. Would you like one?"

"Um, maybe. Anything else on offer?"

Kelly groaned and looked from one to the other. "Goodnight! I'm going to bed. I'll leave you two lovebirds alone." Kelly's footsteps receded and a door clanged shut inside.

Neither Max nor Laura's gaze strayed. He licked his lips. "Now, what I wonder can I tempt you with?"

"Any chocolate?"

He raised an eyebrow. "Only the best. Dark and luscious."

"Well then. What are we waiting for? A girl can only resist so much."

TURNED out her powers of resistance were far more advanced than his own. After an hour of easy conversation and flirtation, Max was finding it increasingly hard to focus on anything other than the way the gauzy material of her dress drifted upward, revealing long, slender legs.

She lay back on the cushions in front of the fire, listening to her favorite David Bowie song, rather than the seductive music he'd tried to play. She'd kicked off her Doc Martens which she seemed to wear with everything, always half undone. Her only jewelry was a long silver chain with a chubby heart locket on it. She fingered it from time to time, with long slender fingers topped by nails that, while neat, weren't painted or manicured to within an inch of their life. She was entirely natural. A natural firebrand, he reminded himself.

He purposely had seated himself the opposite side of the fire. He didn't want to put himself in temptation's way and that was exactly what Laura was—one huge temptation. He knew he had to tread carefully. He might be engaged to her, there might be an undeniable electricity between them, but their arrangement was purely a business one. And he wasn't someone who generally confused the two. Particularly now. Particularly when the stakes were so high.

Plus, while Laura was flirtatious and sexy as hell, he'd seen her give short shrift to a few of the advances the more drunken men had given her, and the not so drunken. It had amused him. She certainly didn't suffer fools gladly, and she certainly wasn't a woman to be crossed. The more time he spent with her, the more attractive she became—and that was saying something, given her impact on him from the instant he'd first set eyes on her.

The coach clock on the mantelpiece chimed and they both looked at it.

"It's three already," said Laura with surprise.

"That early?" he said with a grin. He rose and offered a top up of liqueur. She shook her head. He poured himself another brandy. "You're not tired?"

"No. I'm never tired. I don't sleep for more than five hours anyhow."

"Really? Me neither."

"Sleep is for when you're dead." The word sunk heavily into the atmosphere, immediately changing the mood. She glanced at him, gave a brief, twisted smile and then turned away. "Maybe I will have that drink after all."

He considered her thoughtfully before filling her glass and handing it to her. His fingers brushed hers as she took the glass from him. Her eyes shot wide and met his gaze. He turned away as if it had had no effect on him. He was good at hiding his feelings. He took his seat again. "Are you going to tell me about it?"

She opened her mouth to speak but he could see from the changed expression that she was going to brush off his question. "About what?"

"No," he said. "Don't give me that brush off. Why did you say that about 'sleep being for the dead'. That's not the kind of thing someone would say without a reason."

"Do you think you have some kind of right to ask me personal questions now?"

"Yes. I'm your fiancé, remember."

She shrugged, opened her mouth to speak, sighed and shifted in her seat, suddenly the opposite of relaxed. "Okay. It's the product of experience. I want to live life." She shot him a direct glance, steady once more. "Nothing wrong with that, is there? Surely you don't find that inexplicable?"

He swirled the brandy in the balloon and inhaled its heady fragrance, thinking over her words. Giving himself time, readying himself for an answer. "Living life to the full is all right by me."

"It's the only way."

She took a sip, placed her glass on the stone fireplace and tucked her legs under her. The movement shifted the soft silky stuff of her dress, revealing a flash of tanned thigh and the curve of her behind, before she stood up. She didn't move. The dress hung loosely around her, the silver heart flattening the silk between her breasts. She was intensely sexy, and yet there was an innocence about her sexuality.

Then she came and stood before him. He looked up into her eyes. "What are you doing, Laura?"

"I'm going to kiss you, Max."

"Is that so? And by what right do you do that?" he asked wryly, referring to her earlier comment.

She smiled. "Divine right. I've a feeling your kiss will be

divine."

He smiled but before he could respond, she leaned closer and he felt the warmth and smelled the fragrance of her body as her lips swept his. His heart was pounding as he tried to restrain himself. He gripped the sides of the chair, allowing her to do whatever she wanted. Because she was right. She had a divine right and was completely at liberty to do whatever she wanted with him.

She nudged his nose with hers, and swept the tip of her tongue across his lips before licking her own.

"Interesting. You taste of cherries."

"That's what comes of drinking cherry brandy."

"I love cherries."

"Then you're welcome to another taste."

"Why, thank you."

"Maybe you'd be more comfortable sitting down," he murmured.

She looked around. "The other chair is a long way from yours." She turned back with a smile. "Too far from yours to kiss you."

He shrugged. "You can always sit on my lap—only if you want to, of course. Save your legs." He shrugged. "It's been a long day."

She broke into a smile but the lust never left her eyes. She nodded and slipped onto his lap. He put his arms around her as she nestled against him.

She put her arms around his neck. "Now, where were we?"

He slipped his hand up and caressed her neck before pulling her gently to him. "Right here," he murmured, as he brought her lips to his. She gasped with satisfaction as the kiss deepened. She gave another moan before she pulled away, smiled and briefly brushed her lips once more against his.

"Um, nice." She pushed herself off from his lap and stood, hands on hips, looking down at him. With a smile she walked away, picked up her glass and finished her drink. "Thank you. I'll say goodnight, then."

"Laura," said Max low and husky. "You're surely not going to leave after that."

She turned with a bright smile. "That kiss? Why yes!"

"Don't tell me you didn't enjoy it; don't tell me you don't want more, because I know you do."

"Of course." The way her lips formed the words, still moist and bruised from the kiss, made him even hotter for her. "But I don't always let myself do what I want."

"Any particular reason? Or is it merely to torture some poor unsuspecting male, in this case, unfortunately, me?"

"Yes, there is a reason. I like sensation. I like the moment I feel things intensely. For now, I'm enjoying that feeling of lust, a lust that isn't satisfied. It's the edge of things I'm after. Once I've landed, it's gone." She shrugged. "Nothing seems to live up to that initial feeling. Nothing compares to that feeling of lift-off, of feeling alive. I'm going while I can still feel that sensation humming in my veins."

Max cleared his throat. "I'm glad I came in handy, then. Any time you want to feel lust, you know where to come."

His words were light but he wasn't feeling particularly humorous right at that moment. She chuckled, that low, adorable, heart-stopping chuckle, turned away and walked with her easy grace to the door, opened it and left without saying a further word.

But she didn't bother to close the door and all Max could do was sit and watch as she swayed down the corridor. And all he could think about was that he had six months of marriage in which to give Laura as much sensation as she wanted.

5

"MORE KISSES…MORE OF EVERYTHING? WHAT'S GOING ON, LAURA?" @TELLTALEGIRL #BEHINDCLOSEDDOORS

*T*he next day began, as it had ended. With Laura.

Max shook his head in dismay at his behavior, sitting in front of his big screen, watching her somewhere in Queenstown being interviewed by a reporter. He was dismayed, but not so dismayed that he turned off the computer.

"When's the wedding?" a reporter asked her.

"Saturday!" said Laura with a conviction Max didn't feel. "It's all arranged."

"Is it a white wedding, with all the trimmings?"

"You'll have to be there to find out!" she replied.

"So this *really* is a challenge just like any other?"

Max sat forward, zooming in on her face. If he hadn't, he doubted he would have noticed the slight frown and blink of the eyes.

"No, it's not like any other." She blinked again. "It's harder. It's the most difficult challenge yet."

Max sat back, satisfied. She was honest. He liked that.

"Why harder?"

Laura's face broke out into a grin. "Because there are so

many lovely men out there. It's like being forced to choose from a delicious box of chocolates."

Max huffed, irritated now. He'd effectively been reduced to a caramel creme, or worse still, a Turkish delight.

"So what are you doing in the run-up to the wedding?"

"Max is courting me."

"Starting with?"

"Dinner tonight."

Max reached for his phone. It was turning out to be useful watching Laura on the TV. That way he discovered what was expected of him. True to form, Laura was already deviating from the plans which Chelsey and Kelly had made.

He dialed the Lodge's restaurant. After all, publicizing his Lodge was what this was all about, wasn't it?

"Close off the small restaurant tonight. Yes, all of it. Table for two. No, we'll need the space—there will probably be a dozen or so journalists and cameras around."

A CANDLELIT DINNER, romantic lighting, exquisite food and wine, and beautiful company—it was the epitome of a romantic evening date. Except for the journalists.

Turned out that a dozen was a vast underestimate. The word had spread and up to thirty journalists and sight-seers jostled for space around the entrance and in the gardens of the restaurant. But Max ignored them because he couldn't take his eyes off Laura, who was dressed up for once, in a shimmering dress with more sparkles than material. Her blonde hair had been straightened and makeup applied. But Laura looked nervous and rubbed her eyes.

"You've just spoiled your makeup," Max observed.

"Bugger!" She licked her finger and swept it under her eyes, spreading the black mascara in a sweeping arc under her eye. "Better?" She leaned forward, wide-eyed in a girlish way which made him smile.

"Better if you're a panda, maybe."

She sipped her wine and crossed her arms on the table. "Kelly persuaded me to play dress up. I knew I shouldn't."

"Play dress up? How old are you? Twelve?"

"At heart, yes," she replied without a trace of irony.

"Really?" He leaned forward and camera flashes lit up the darkness outside the window. They ignored them. "You felt quite mature last night."

She looked up at him warily and there was another blast of flashes, eager to capture any sense of doubt in their heroine's face. "I'm not usually like that."

"Yes, I could sense that, too."

"You could?"

"Um. You're certainly not your average..." He stopped abruptly, suddenly realizing he didn't know enough about her to complete the sentence. "I don't know how old you are."

She shrugged. "I'm not surprised. We really don't know much about each other at all."

"Then maybe this is a good occasion to remedy that. How about we forget all the other stuff, let's begin again, pretend tonight is our first date. A regular date, like normal people have."

She smiled, the first relaxed smile of the evening. "That sounds good to me. Where shall we start?"

"Ladies first."

"I'm not often called a lady."

"My mother brought me up to respect women. You're a lady in my book."

"That's cool. I like it. Okay, I'm twenty-two years of age and I was born in London, moved to LA when I was twelve."

"Ah, I wondered at the mid-Atlantic accent."

"My mother was British, my father, American."

"Do they move around a lot for work?"

"They move *constantly* for work. My father is a diplomat, as was my mother when they met. But she gave up work when she had me."

"Only child?"

She grinned. "How did you guess?"

"Stab in the dark." He grinned back. There was something irresistible about this woman's inability to take herself seriously. "So how come you went from only child to daredevil?"

The grin faded from her face and she picked up her fork and pushed her salad around before looking up at him again. "Something happened."

He cocked his head to one side. "Go on."

She paused. "Max, I'm going to tell you something I usually keep pretty quiet. I *can* trust you, can't I?"

Again that beguiling naiveté—that she would trust him on the basis of him saying he was trustworthy.

"Yes, you can. You can tell me anything and it won't go any further."

She nodded. "I thought I could. I'm a pretty good judge of character." She sighed. "Anyway, my father was working as a diplomat in the Far East, in Cambodia, when it happened."

She paused and swallowed. He hadn't seen her looking nervous before, but the evidence was there, in the way she averted her eyes, and in the way she fiddled with the napkin.

"Go on," he said quietly, instinctively knowing this was something important to her, something she needed to tell him.

She took a deep breath. "I came home from school one day—a private international school, you understand. My parents were out and out snobs and kept me apart from normal people as much as they could. Which"—her eyes sparkled mischievously—"admittedly wasn't that much. I used to get away."

"I can't imagine anyone keeping *you* caged for long."

"No, well, their plan of keeping me away from the locals never worked. I used to play hooky, checking out the markets, making friends with the local kids. But it backfired on me when I came home from school one day with a mystery illness."

He frowned. Of all the things coming, he hadn't imagined this. "What illness?"

"No one knew for a long time. They thought I was making it up. But why would a seventeen-year-old who loved nothing better than waiting until everyone was in bed before sneaking out the window and getting into trouble, make up the fact that she couldn't move out of bed?"

"Couldn't move? What? Not at all?"

"A little. But as soon as I got out of bed, I collapsed again. I was exhausted. And my joints were all swollen and painful." She frowned tensely. "I went from being a normal energetic teenager to this useless invalid. Everything had to be done for me. It was humiliating *and* terrifying. Watching the world move around me but unable to respond or join in."

"How long were you like that?"

"Four months at my worst. Felt like four years," she said bleakly, looking out, beyond him, into a past which still had the power to terrify. "Then more months on top of that when I was confined to the house."

"What was it?"

"Rheumatic fever—a disease which had obviously surfaced in the markets where I used to hang out when Mom and Dad thought I was at school."

"How long did it take for you to recover?"

"Around a year, I guess."

"That must have been hard."

"Yes. I wanted to die."

He reached out and took her hand. There was another volley of flashing lights and they both jumped, having forgotten where they were. He turned his gaze back to her, not letting go of her hand. "Go on."

"It was only my computer that kept me going. Dad still had work and traveled a lot and Mom had to go with him to do all that entertaining bullshit they did. To be honest, I don't think it was a hard decision for Mom to make. She wasn't very domesticated. I guess we're alike there. No, it was the staff who cared for me. And Kelly. She's been my best friend since forever and I couldn't have got through it without her. She made them rig up a computer on the wall and I had touch controls. I lived my life through YouTube. And I vowed, *vowed*"—she repeated the word with such emphasis that he knew just how important this experience must have been to her—"to live my life to the fullest—to feel and experience everything the world has to offer, just as my heroes and heroines who'd kept me going through that dark year had done. For myself and for others like me."

He squeezed the hand he still held. "I had no idea."

"No, for all that I live my life in the public eye, I haven't revealed anything of my past. I prefer it that way. And I covered my tracks pretty good. No one's been able to discover anything about my past, and they've tried, believe me."

"I bet they have. So, as far as everyone's concerned, you've emerged, a fully formed YouTube star."

"Yes. As soon as I could manage it I was in the gym, training every day and when I could, I left home and I've never been back."

"What, never?"

"No, why would I? I never want to see the inside of that bedroom again."

"And your parents?"

She shrugged. "I see them from time to time, whenever we're in the same city."

"And what do they think about what you do?"

She shrugged and avoided his eye. "We don't talk about it. 'Some things, Laura'"—she assumed a posh English accent—"'are best left unsaid.' That's my Mom, the epitome of English restraint."

"You must take after your dad then."

"God knows who I take after. When I was little I read a book about faeries who'd leave children on the doorsteps of people who wanted children. For years I truly thought I was one of them. All the faeries in the picture book were blonde and both my parents are dark. I used to look out the window, trying to see if the faeries had come to visit to see if I was okay." She grunted. "But they never came." She twisted her lips. "And I wasn't okay. I felt a misfit at home from when I was very young. And when I was ill, I hated it."

"But you're completely well now, aren't you?"

She nodded but drained her glass of wine too quickly before holding it out to the waiter who was hovering close by. "That is *really* good wine."

"*Are* you completely well, now, Laura?" Max repeated. She shrugged and thanked the waiter before turning back to Max, who hadn't shifted his gaze from her. He was going to get an answer to his question, if he had to sit there all night, repeating it. "Laura?"

"I"—she exhaled—"sustained injuries… scars."

He frowned as he tried to remember the side effects of rheumatic fever. Then he remembered and he looked hard at her. He licked his lips. "Your heart?"

She nodded. "The valves. Scarred." She shrugged and looked around, obviously trying to find something to distract him. "It's fine though."

He reached out to her. There was no way he was going to be distracted from this. "So how come you're doing all this physical stuff? Pushing yourself to the limit? Isn't it dangerous?"

She shrugged. "The valves are working fine. They're just scarred." She shrugged and shot him a bright smile. "Anyhow, I don't want to talk about this anymore. It is what it is. And I don't want you to mention it. Please."

It was as if icy cold liquid had been poured down his spine, as he sat there, holding the hand of a woman who all the world saw as untouchable. She wasn't. The world had touched her, she'd responded and he'd make sure he'd continue to touch her, as he was, now, holding her hand, willing his strength into her. Because, like it or not, she wasn't the strong woman everyone saw. She was young, vulnerable, and scared. He could feel it in the way she curled her fingers around his hand, gripping him hard. *Very* scared.

"Isn't there anything that can be done? No treatment to be had?"

"No. It's fine." She grimaced, awkward at opening up to him. "The tests showed scarring but nothing so bad it needed surgery. It should be fine. And, if it's not, then I'll deal with it then."

"But your doctors, specialists, when you see them—"

"I don't see them."

"You what?"

She shrugged. "There's no way I'm going back into hospital. What's the point?"

"To see if there's any change? To see if everything is okay?"

"I'm fine. I *feel* fine. *Everything's* fine. Believe me, every day I don't see a doctor or a hospital is a good day. All I want to do is enjoy life." She held up her wine to him. "Cheers! Here's to life!"

Max clinked his glass to hers. The light was bright in her eyes once more.

"So that's my happy little story," she continued. "Your turn now."

There was so much more Max wanted to know, so much more he wanted to find out about this woman, who not only excited him, but had touched him in a way that stirred his most protective instincts. But now wasn't the time. Telling him that much had been hard for her. He smiled. "What would you like to know?"

"Age?"

"Thirty-one."

"Family?"

"Three brothers, three sisters. I had another brother, Jonny, who died a year ago. My father lives in the family home outside Akaroa, near Christchurch."

"Wow, the Connelly family is big."

"Yeah. And crazy, too. Most of them."

"You don't seem particularly crazy to me." She gestured around. "You own a big, flash alpine resort, drive an expensive car, fly a helicopter. Sounds pretty focused to me."

"You've been doing your homework."

She laughed. "You don't think I'm about to marry someone without doing due diligence."

"Due diligence," he repeated. "I guess such an unemotional expression sums up what our marriage is about."

"Unemotional? Fun is an emotion, excitement, fear of the unknown. That's what I want out of this. Don't you?"

"Sure. Perhaps less of the fear, though. But..." He hesitated. "Don't you ever want to feel anything more than fun and excitement?"

"Like what?"

He held her gaze but couldn't tell whether she was being deliberately obtuse or truly hadn't thought of marriage as encompassing any other form of emotion. He looked over at the photographers who hadn't let up their attention. He really didn't want to see any photos of him plastered around the internet with the word 'love' hovering on his lips.

"How about we leave this feeding frenzy behind?"

"I don't eat that badly, do I?" she asked with a grin.

He laughed. "You know what I mean." He jerked his head toward the group of photographers. "*Their* frenzy, *their* feeding."

She turned back to him with a cheeky twist of the lips. "Let's give them something to take away first, shall we?"

"Take away? Do people always want to take something from you?"

"Yes." She shrugged. "It's part of the job."

"Hm." He raised an eyebrow. "So what did you have in mind?"

She placed her napkin on the table and stood up, the figure-hugging black dress, covered in crystal beading, shimmered under the lights. Her blonde hair, longer now it was straightened, swept over one shoulder, brushing her breast. A single black jade dangly earring was revealed on the exposed earlobe. Her plum-colored lipstick and flawless complexion was offset by the still-smudged mascara. His gaze fell to those lips, curved into a delicious sensuous half-smile. His single thought was making sure the lipstick became just as smudged as the mascara by the end of the evening.

He rose and she hooked her arm into his. "Over to you on this one. I'm out of my depth here."

"No problem," she whispered in his ear, causing his skin to goose-bump.

She took his hand and, chatting happily, for all the world like the perfect couple, they walked toward the photographers.

"Hey guys!" she said. "I hope you've already eaten, because if you haven't, you must be hungry hanging around watching us eat."

Max had to admire her sweetness with the group. They obviously knew her well and she, them, and chatted easily. He realized why they'd kept a respectful distance. They loved her and, within the constraints of their job, did what they could to give her some space.

"Well, we're off now. You guys have a good evening."

"Come on, Laura!" shouted a photographer.

She turned. "Okay. Ready?" She placed her palm on one side of his cheek and turned him to face her. She rose on tiptoes until her lips met his. He didn't respond immediately and he saw a flicker of something like alarm flit across her features. Then he slid his finger through her hair, bunching it in his hand, and brought her face to his and kissed her in no uncertain terms. He was sure that she'd only meant a brief pressing of lips together. But that wasn't his idea of a kiss. And certainly bore no relation to what he'd imagined doing to that lipstick all evening.

But even *his* idea of a kiss became lost as it intensified. As her mouth opened under his and he slid his tongue along hers he felt her gasp in his mouth. From that moment he lost any idea of time and place. It was only when he heard the not-so-discreet cough of Chelsey, followed by her instructions to the photographers to leave, that the show was over. He even heard the remonstrations from the photographers that it looked like the show was only about to begin, without any shift of focus.

It was Laura who eventually pulled away. He saw why when he opened his eyes. Kelly had effectively dragged her away.

He also saw that he'd managed to smudge that perfect lipstick, just as he'd imagined he would. Trouble was it, it only had the effect of making him want more. It wasn't so much a mission accomplished, as a mission only just begun.

"Come on you two," said Chelsey. "Time you took your party somewhere private." She turned to Kelly. "Time for a quick meeting?"

"Sure," said Kelly.

As they stepped outside into the balmy evening, Max turned to Laura, whose hand had somehow slipped into his. "Something tells me that our employees are trying to figure out how to handle us."

"Oh, yes. They'll come up with something."

"You don't mind your public life being run by someone else?"

"No." Laura looked genuinely surprised at the suggestion.

"Just wondered."

"Do you?"

"Chelsey doesn't run my life," he said quickly. Then he reflected. "She just tries to put it in order."

"Not surprised if you keep pulling stunts like that one." She rubbed her finger along her lips.

He stopped walking. "*Me* pulling stunts? You were setting *me* up. I was beginning to feel like a used man." He grinned. "I couldn't have that."

"Why not?"

"Because, Laura, I may respect women, I may think they're better than me in many ways, but I still like to take control."

It was dark, with only the stars above as light. They were around the back of the building, with no one else in sight. "And what if I don't like you taking control?"

He cocked his head to one side. "You didn't seem to mind too much back there."

"I…" She faltered. She shrugged, the whites of her eyes shifting in confusion under the starlight.

He took hold of her chin and brought her gently round to face him. "Laura, admit it. For a while there you forgot to be the director of your life, forgot all about control, and let your body take the lead."

"I might have done," she said hesitantly.

"You sound unsure. Maybe I'd better show you again."

"No—" But wherever she was going to say was robbed as he pressed his lips to hers. The sound morphed into a moan. And, as her hands snaked around his neck, her fingers pushed up into his hair, she settled against his chest and then his hips.

His body reacted instantly to her taut, lean body pressed hard against his. He could tell the moment she felt his response—it would have been hard to ignore. For some reason it was different to the previous night. Then she'd been on familiar territory—flirting with no thought to the future beyond a few days. But now? Now she froze for an instant before drawing back from him, her eyes naked. Gone was the bravado for the public, the laughter for the friends, instead there was uncertainty and… fear.

It took all his restraint to step away with a smile. "This is your room, I believe." Still that look in her eye that shot to the heart of him. "Goodnight, Laura."

It wasn't his arousal with which he had to struggle as he turned from her, but his need to wipe away that fear and uncertainty. He hadn't seen it in her eyes before and it shocked him. It took all his strength to walk away. Now wasn't the time. And he suddenly realized that, even if he never saw her again after their marriage ended, he had to help her overcome the fear which she hid so well.

He waited until he heard her door open and close before entering his room. He opened the curtains and saw her light turn on and then out. He got his phone from his pocket and checked the time. It was late but his brother had always been a night owl. He tapped the screen.

"Gabe! How are you, mate?" He listened briefly and grinned. His brother knew him inside out. "You're right. I do want something, but it's not for me. What do you know about rheumatic fever?"

~

THE PHONE RANG AGAIN and Max glanced at it with irritation. He picked it up and checked the display. Another sister.

He took a deep breath and tapped the screen. "Rachel!" he said with all the heartiness he could muster after having listened not only to Lizzi, but to his brothers have a go at him. Even his youngest sister, Amber, the free-and-easy, live and let live hippy, had given him an earful.

"You're insane!" said Rachel.

"Lovely to hear from you, too!" he replied, scrolling through his emails and deleting as he went. He may as well make himself useful while he was subjected to the telling-off his sister was about to give him.

"I love you, Max, and I'm telling you you're insane! Imagine what everyone else is saying."

"I don't *care* what anyone else is saying."

"Could have fooled me! I thought that's what this whole stunt is about—what everyone else thinks." She paused, obviously waiting for a comeback. He decided not to give her one. "Lizzi told me that you'd told her that it's a publicity stunt. Say she's wrong, Max?"

He bit his lip and deleted a couple of more emails which he didn't bother to read. He hoped they weren't important. He pushed his chair back and rose and paced over to the window. Camera flashes ensued and he swore under his breath. He was about to close the blinds but left them. It was too late for that. He'd opened his life up to public scrutiny and he'd have to accept it.

"Lizzi isn't wrong."

Rachel groaned.

"Rachel, you have to understand, Laura and I aren't like you guys. It's just a stunt. Nothing more. It's simply marriage. It doesn't mean anything to either of us."

"Then it should!" Rachel exploded. "Christ, Max! What would Mum say?"

He felt the stab of the dagger she'd thrust, deep inside. "This is between Laura and me, no one else."

"Just you two, and the rest of the world."

A heavy silence fell which told him more than words. It spoke of a disappointment which hurt him more than anything else she had to say.

"I have to go," he said.

"Of course," she said shortly. "Have you spoken to Dad?"

"Dad?" He twisted around, frowning at the thought. He pushed his fingers through his hair. "Dad," he groaned. He hadn't thought about his father's reaction to the news. And Rachel's earful would be nothing to what his father's would be. He and his father had never seen eye to eye. Not as a kid, not as an adult, and definitely not now.

"Yes, *Dad*. As in your father. Call him."

Rachel finished the call before he did and he ended up listening to silence, before tossing the phone onto the desk. He looked at it again. He should call his father. Of course he should. He was getting married in two days and he hadn't even spoken to his father about it. He walked over and picked up the phone, weighing it in his hands, tossing it from one hand to the other.

There was a knock at the door and it opened. Chelsey's assistant smiled brightly. "Chelsey said to tell you that we're ready for you."

He placed the phone deliberately on the desk. "Sure." His father would have to wait. He had a wedding to organize.

HE WAS glad that none of his sisters were here to witness this, he thought as he closed the door on the board room. He rarely used this formal room, keeping it for conferences and residential meetings which they organized. But here he was, seated beside Chelsey and her assistant on his other side, facing Laura and her friend and manager, Kelly.

At least Laura looked as uncomfortable as he felt. She sat like a child called into the headmaster's office, fiddling with her phone. Obviously the romantic side of this business wasn't called for here, in private.

"So," said Chelsey, striding up to the whiteboard and uncapping a marker. "Kelly and I have begun organizing things. We have a wedding planner on to the gown, flowers, photos, all of that regular crap."

Max blanched at the use of the word 'crap', remembering Rachel's jibe about his mother. He felt doubly bad as he also felt responsible for Chelsey's attitude to marriage. At one time, Chelsey had wanted to marry him and he'd refused. It had spelled the end of their intimate relationship and, apparently, the end of Chelsey's marriage ambitions. He suddenly realized that his spur-of-the-moment proposal was affecting more people than he'd thought. If he'd thought at all, he reflected glumly.

"The ring will have to stay on Laura's finger," said Kelly. "We'll fudge that in the ceremony. And I've found some vows on the internet which you might like to take a look at." She pushed a piece of paper along the table to Laura. But Laura didn't bother looking at it. She pushed it across to Chelsey and continued texting. "Laura!" said Kelly.

"Aren't you interested in what you're going to say on your big day?"

Laura looked up with a slightly dazed expression on her face, as if she'd been miles away. "No. Why would I be?" She looked across at Max. "Are you?"

He shrugged. "I don't want to say anything I don't mean."

Chelsey scanned the page. "You won't. This is just general stuff. You know, respect, blah, blah."

He crossed his legs. He was growing more uncomfortable by the minute. "Sounds fine then." How had he got himself into a situation where he was saying the opposite to how he felt? He never did that.

"Our strategy is going to be that we make everything as flashy as possible and say as little as possible. That way you guys won't incriminate yourself, but will do what everyone wants."

"Put on a show for them," said Laura under her breath, as she continued to send tweets around the world. So she *was* listening, then. He found it hard to reconcile the woman who sat there—allowing herself to be talked about, to be used as an object for all their businesses—with the woman he'd been with last night. But then he reflected, what she'd told him the previous night had shown a different side to her. He watched as her hair slipped over her face. She was wearing cut-off shorts and a gypsy blouse which fell from her shoulders, revealing tanned and taut muscles, and a long elegant neck. It hurt to see such beauty and such indifference. It hurt to see how scared she was and how she was hiding it from the rest of the world.

"Laura?" His voice was low and quiet but everyone stopped talking and Laura's fingers stopped tapping her phone. She bit her lip and looked up, her expression naked and suddenly vulnerable. "Are you sure you want to go through with this? You don't have to, you know. You don't have to do anything you don't want to do."

He was rewarded when a flicker of gratitude and warmth crossed her face. "Thank you, but it's okay."

Kelly and Chelsey raised their eyebrows and exchanged relieved looks.

"Of course it's okay," said Chelsey. "Don't worry, Max. It'll be fine. It'll be over before you know it."

Max held Laura's gaze. "Over before you know it," he repeated. "A marriage made in heaven," he added wryly.

Laura's lips quirked with amusement. "Or hell," she said, looking back down at her phone.

6

"WEDDING BELLS ARE RINGING! TILL SIX MONTHS US DO PART?" @TELLTALEGIRL #THEULTIMATECHALLENGE

*L*aura had hardly stopped during the three days of preparation leading up to her wedding. She'd had a prior commitment in Fiordland, panning for gold underwater, which had kept her busy, but even when she was forced to stay put she was either on the phone, the computer, or talking to people. And that was exactly how she liked it. It didn't give her time to think and she really didn't want time to reflect on what she was about to do. Telltale Girl was right —this was her biggest challenge yet.

But now she and Kelly had returned to Queenstown Lodge, nerves had kicked in big time. It was the morning of her wedding and there was no distraction to be found anywhere—not on her phone and certainly not with the dressmaker making last minute adjustments to the hemline of her wedding dress, and Kelly talking her through the wedding arrangements.

Laura scrolled through her Twitter feed as she stood on the coffee table while the dressmaker pinned up her hem. "Telltale Girl sounds really keen to see me hitched."

"Will you leave that phone alone, Laura!" growled Kelly. "Let the dressmaker do her job."

Laura sighed and tossed the phone onto the sofa. "Okay?" she asked Kelly. "Sorry," she said to the dressmaker, who mumbled a response through a mouthful of pins.

While Kelly and the dressmaker fussed around her, Laura stood, hands by her sides as she'd been instructed and, without diversion, her mind drifted to Max—something she'd been trying to avoid since their last kiss. That kiss... it had taken her to places which she'd only read about. What was worse than an arranged marriage? An arranged marriage with someone she really liked. She sighed and fidgeted and the dressmaker tutted.

It was ridiculous, weird, incomprehensible, but with each meeting with Max her discomfort increased. It was a charade and usually she was comfortable with charades, but when her partner-in-crime looked at her with such a toe-curling sensuousness that her tummy flipped with desire, she suddenly found herself looking at herself through *his* eyes, and not liking what he was seeing, not liking what she'd become.

She didn't want him to think she was a shallow adrenaline junkie with no ideas or thoughts or feelings beyond the immediate need to have fun. It must have been this notion which made her reveal her childhood illness to him, something only a few people knew. She couldn't think of any other reason. She still couldn't believe she'd told him so much about herself.

No, he wasn't the usual two-dimensional acquaintance with whom she flirted briefly before moving on. He was a man who interested her, who had feelings, a past and a family, someone who drew her in before she could say, "self-preservation".

"There." The dressmaker smoothed down the already sleek folds of her dress, stood back and looked inquiringly at Kelly.

Kelly formed her fingers in an approving "O". "Perfect!" She rose and walked around Laura as if she were a statue in an art gallery. "So, what do you think, Laura?"

Laura looked down at her dress. It was beautiful, no doubt about that. While the cream satin draped around her curves in a way that was designed to make sure all eyes were on her, it wasn't big and flouncy and over the top, her only request. Trouble was, she had the uncomfortable feeling that she was a prize, wrapped up and about to be presented to the highest bidder. Stupid. It was her decision. She'd accepted the proposal, the challenge, whatever the hell it was called. She sighed and focused on the dress.

"It's lovely. Thanks for not giving me a crinoline. This is beautiful. It's very…" Words failed her. She'd never given a moment's thought to wedding dresses before, let alone needed to describe one.

"Sweet and sexy, is what it is," said Kelly.

"Sweet and sexy, yes. Thanks," Laura said to the dressmaker.

"If you leave your account at reception, we'll see it's paid," said Kelly dismissing the woman.

Laura sat, her full cream satin gown bunched up around her knees, and twirled the stiletto shoe around in her hand by its heel. She'd never before worn shoes like these either. She didn't know if she *could* wear them, let along walk in them.

She turned it over—cool color though: the sole was fuchsia pink, the top a creamy satin to match the dress.

She held it up to Kelly. "I can't wear these! I'll trip up on that lovely pink carpet you have rolled out for me."

Kelly didn't even look up from inspecting the flowers—long stemmed white lilies. She gave the okay to the florist who scurried off to get everything in place.

Laura slipped one shoe on. "At least it fits."

Kelly grinned. "You *shall* go to the ball, Cinderella."

Laura glowered at her and wrinkled her nose. The heavy scent of lilies filled the air. Wearing only one shoe, she limped across to the other side of the room and pushed open the windows and took a deep breath. There was a hint of autumn in the air. The deciduous trees in the valley had turned brilliant shades of orange, red and yellow and there was a slight chill now at night.

She rested her arms on the sill, still twirling the other shoe in her hand out the window. Kelly came up behind her and grabbed it from her. "Do you know how much that cost?"

Laura sighed. "No."

"And I don't suppose you care, either," Kelly grumbled, as she checked the clipboard which appeared to be permanently attached to her hand.

Laura poked her head further out the window. She could just see the fuchsia carpet rolling toward the raised dais where she and Max would say their vows. She gulped at the thought. White flowers were everywhere, with bright dashes of the same pink as the carpet evident in the swags which held back the floaty white curtains and in the small posies which adorned the back of each seat. White and pink everywhere. The effect was elegant and glamorous—everything Laura wasn't.

Kelly turned to Laura, her irritation evident on her face. "Try on the other shoe, for goodness' sake, and practice your walk."

Grumbling, Laura slipped the other shoe on and rose,

slightly stooped. She glanced at Kelly who sighed and shook her head.

"Are you telling me that jumping off the side of mountains on a bike, free-falling out of aeroplanes, bungy jumping, eating live insects, none of this bothers you more than walking in high heels?"

Laura pouted—something she didn't know she could do —and tried to stand taller. She could do this. She found her balance and walked, one step in front of the other. She focused on a painting at the end of the room and fixed on it as her target as she walked toward it. She turned around with a sense of achievement and saw Kelly nearly doubled up laughing.

"You walk like a drag queen."

"Gee, thanks very much!"

"Actually not as good as a drag queen—they walk better than most women. You walk like a man in stilettos."

Laura sat down and pulled off her shoes, trying to keep at bay a feeling which was alien to her—defeat. "I can't do this."

"You can and you will. It wasn't me who accepted this challenge, it was *you*. And, unless you want to be the laughing stock of thousands of people—"

"Millions at the last count—"

"Then you'd better get back to practising your walk."

Kelly's phone rang and she answered it while Laura walked up and down the room a few times.

Kelly glanced at her, put her hand over the phone. "Stand straight and flex your bottom muscles." She sighed after another few steps. "My mom used to tell me to imagine someone's pulling a string up through you, out of your head."

Laura continued to practice. "I don't need to be told that —someone's already pulling a string."

Kelly finished her conversation and crossed her arms. "You mean me?"

Laura shook her head, bunched up the gown around her hips and sat down. This whole business was getting more and more depressing. "Not you. I know I'm doing it to myself. It's just…" She sighed.

Kelly shot her a sharp glance. "What's up?"

"Nothing."

"*Yes*-thing. I haven't seen that look in a long time," she said more kindly, coming up to Laura. "Spill."

"It's just all of this. It's not me."

"Come on. Somewhere in your unromantic past there must have been a time when you imagined yourself in this situation."

"What? About to marry someone I've only met a few times? No, I can honestly say that I've never imagined a scenario like this one."

"I don't mean that. I mean getting married in a general sense. You know, committing to one person for the rest of your life. A girl's big day. Even *I've* day-dreamed of getting married." Kelly sorted through some accounts and drew her laptop toward her. "Walking down the aisle with my father, everyone looking at me, my man standing at the altar." Kelly sat back in her chair and gazed into the mid-distance. "He has hair that's too long, and sits on his white shirt collar." She raised her hands and indicated the back of her neck. "Just there. Just right." She sighed.

Laura frowned. "You're talking about Jack, aren't you?"

A blushing Kelly tapped at her laptop without looking up. "Jack?" she said with a distracted air. "Jack who?"

Laura slid off her chair and walked across to Kelly, looking over her shoulder. Kelly's hands paused. "You know who. Seems you haven't gotten over him like you claim."

Kelly's lips twisted but she kept her eyes down, glued to the keyboard, her fingers unmoving. She cleared her throat and looked into Laura's direct gaze. "Of course I have. I was talking of adolescent dreams. Don't tell me you didn't have them. No weddings?"

"Yes, weddings. A long time ago. Nothing fancy like yours, or like this. But any thoughts of one has been long-since buried."

"When you got sick."

"Yep. *I* might have survived, but some parts of me didn't. The romantic part, the part that thought I'd have a future like any other girl."

Kelly raised her hand and took Laura's and squeezed it. "Come on. Don't get maudlin on me. That's not like you. Look at the facts. You're marrying someone totally hot."

"True. What else?"

"There doesn't need to *be* anything else. A totally hot man more than compensates for anything else lacking."

"Do you really think I can do this?"

Kelly hugged Laura. "Sweetie, I know you can. Just another challenge, remember. Just another challenge"—she glanced at her watch and her expression changed to one of panic—"which is going to begin in a few short hours!"

As Kelly charged off, Laura groaned and put her head in her hands, just as the sounds of a string quartet started up. How come getting married terrified her more than saddle bronc riding at a rodeo?

TWO HOURS LATER, Laura peeped out from behind the marquee flap and scanned the scene before her. The garden was awash with beautiful people. It was close to mid-day— the time set for her to emerge—and the cool of the morning had disappeared, leaving the day bright and clear. The women had been asked to wear a fuchsia pink accessory and the result was a stunning vision when combined with the dark suits and white shirts of the men. Kelly had always teased her about her favorite color being pink when Laura was such a tomboy and now Laura was beginning to think she'd changed her mind. The pink blazed at her like a reproach as she looked around with increasing nerves, increasing queasiness.

She let the marquee flap drop and turned to Kelly who was going through a checklist with the wedding planner. "How long do I have to wait?" Laura knew she sounded petulant and unreasonable, but she indulged herself anyway.

Kelly threw her an amused look. "Not used to being out of the spotlight, are you?"

"It's not that…" Laura sat on the chair and the satin slipped down her bare legs. She shrugged. "It's waiting I'm not used to. It makes me nervous."

Kelly threw her head back and laughed. "You? Nervous?" She walked over to her and the laughter faded. "You're not kidding, are you?" She frowned. "Look, five minutes and then you'll be out there. Do you regret this? You don't have to go through with it, you know. Not if you don't want to."

Laura rolled her eyes. "Right. I'll just pop out there, call the whole thing off, and watch my 'career' fall into ruins. And not just mine. Yours, too." She gestured to Kelly's assistant and others who helped her do what she did. "And all the rest. There'd be no money coming in to pay for their salaries." She suddenly felt the crushing sense of obligation, that came with this behemoth of a career she'd invented for herself. She'd thought she was having fun, chasing freedom. What she hadn't realized was that she was setting her own trap. There and then she decided she'd have to do something about it. But not here. Not now. "No. I've committed to this. I'll go ahead." She jumped up and looked away from Kelly, not wanting to see the relief on her face.

"Good." But Laura could hear the relief in her voice. "Now, let's have a good look at you." She smoothed down the satin as Laura slipped her shoes on her bare feet.

"You should have worn stockings. Or at least a garter."

"I draw the line at garters and I hate stockings. Besides, I was worried I'd slip out of these shoes. With bare feet at least I can grip them."

"Just hold on to me as we go down the aisle—I mean carpet—and you'll be fine."

Laura gnawed her lip. "Are you sure?"

Kelly gave her a hug. "Sure I'm sure." She tried to turn Laura toward the mirror, but she didn't budge. "Just look at you. You're gorgeous. That's all that's required of you today —looking gorgeous and not falling off your shoes. How hard can that be?"

Very hard, Kelly, very hard. But Laura didn't voice her thoughts. Instead, she stood with her back to the mirror as the hairdresser made some last minute adjustments. Laura had insisted on her hair being natural, but from the amount of lotions and spray the hairdresser was applying, Laura somehow doubted her wishes had been taken into consideration. At least the flowers were real. Laura had no idea how she was going to end up looking and she was beyond caring. Any idea of control over the day was long gone.

"You should have got your parents over here," said Kelly.

"You're kidding! They're mad enough with me anyway. They don't need to know."

"Um, don't you think they might hear?"

Laura shrugged. "I doubt it. They're both so wrapped up in their own world, I don't think they even know my YouTube channel exists. And I'm positive they've never heard of Twitter. Anyway I want *you* to give me away. You've been by my side watching out for me for as long as I can remember."

Kelly's face softened. "And I'm going to continue to watch out for you—married or not!" She gave her a hug. "Now, all set? Let's have a look at you." Kelly smiled. "You'll do."

Laura took a deep breath and nodded.

"You haven't even looked in the mirror."

Reluctantly, Laura turned around and did a double take, peering at the person she scarcely recognized. She raised her eyebrows in disbelief. Only when her reflection followed suit, did she accept the fact that this was the new Laura. She walked up to the mirror. "What the hell have you done to me? I hardly recognize myself."

Kelly pulled her away. "That's because you don't look in the mirror often enough. You're such a tomboy. Your looks are completely wasted on you."

Laura shrugged and her reflection shrugged back. "This is turning into the weirdest day. I don't think I've ever felt more nervous."

"You look beautiful, that's all you need worry about. Now, take a deep breath, okay?"

Laura took hold of Kelly's hands and inhaled slowly, copying Kelly. Just as she did before each challenge, just as she'd done when they were teenagers together, when Laura had needed all the calm and strength and support that Kelly could give her to carry on. But this time was different and Laura could see Kelly knew it.

"Come here," said Kelly, pulling Laura into her arms and hugging her. "You can do it, you know. Just another challenge. Just something else to make you feel alive, something different to experience."

Laura swallowed down the nerves. She pressed her lips together as she felt them tremble but met Kelly's strong gaze. "Right."

The strains of music changed, and turned into the wedding march.

Kelly peeped out from behind the tent flap. "Max is there, and his best man—never seen him before." She glanced at Laura. "It's time."

"God, Kelly, what the hell am I doing?"

"What are you doing? Getting married, of course."

Laura took a deep breath and slipped on her shoes. Kelly offered her arm and Laura took a few faltering steps towards her.

"You can hold on to me while we walk. Then all you have to do is stand there. And, after you're married, you can hold onto Max. So don't worry about those shoes."

"They're coming off as soon as I'm done," whispered Laura, as the curtains swept open. Everyone turned and gasped.

"Showtime," said Kelly, like a ventriloquist with a wide smile on her face.

Laura turned to see everyone looking at her and for the first time in her life felt shy. She tightened her grip on Kelly and took a step forward. The dress fell in easy waves around her body, higher at the front so there was no possibility of tripping. As they stepped out from the protection of the marquee, a murmur of appreciation spread around the guests like a ripple. Laura was thankful for Kelly's reassuring presence, anchoring her into the moment. Time seemed to slow, and she was aware of only snatches of images—of a woman's hat, slicing against the blue sky in brilliant vermillion; of a child's bright eyes looking up at her from the feet of her mother; and of the pink and white rose petals which had been strewn on the carpet before her. The spell was only broken when she looked up and caught Max's gaze. He was staring at her as if he'd never seen her before, as if she was someone different—someone feminine and sophisticated. If she could fool Max, maybe she could do this—maybe she could even fool herself.

Then he smiled at her, as if to reassure her. She smiled back, more relaxed now, and glanced at Kelly who squeezed her hand as they continued up the carpet.

She gained confidence with every step of her beautiful pink-soled shoes. She smiled at the cameras pointed at her. She waved toward the back, behind the rows of seats, to where a group of young people gathered who'd followed her here from Australia. They waved back excitedly. Then she looked forward once more and saw she was within a few steps of Max.

The surprised expression had given way to a more guarded one now. But it was still warm, hot even. He offered his arm. Laura let go of Kelly and slotted her hand through Max's arm in a relaxed stance. Together they both turned and smiled at the sea of cameras before turning back to each other.

Laura raised her eyebrows and gave a brief grimace, trying to lighten the situation. He inclined his head to hers. "Are you okay? You looked a bit nervous back there."

"I'm fine now, thanks." And, as they turned to the marriage celebrant, she realized she was. She glanced at Kelly who nodded encouragingly.

Laura remembered their practice run and turned to face Max. They'd stepped up onto a dais with the marriage celebrant to her left, facing the crowds who spilled out from the seated area to the gardens beyond. Still more people hung out the windows, watching. Max took both her hands in his and swept his thumb over the back of hers, obviously aware of the slight tremble in her limbs.

The celebrant spoke and she recognized the words which Kelly and Chelsey had chosen. They were more romantic than Laura had imagined, but they did the job. And that, she reminded herself, was exactly what it was—a job. But a surreal job. She felt as if she were above it, looking down on it all. That this was happening to someone else, not her.

In order to try to stay focused, she stared fixedly at Max's face. He had good bone structure—the clean, sharp lines of his jaw, his nose, his brow—all softened by sensual lips. She felt a soft flutter, low in her belly, as she remembered the effect of those lips when pressed against hers. Involuntarily she licked them and was aware of the heat, building within the confines of the natural amphitheater.

Suddenly there was silence and those lips which she couldn't take her eyes off, quirked into a smile. There was a pressure on her hands and she looked up into Max's eyes. He nodded encouragingly. She glanced at the celebrant.

"What?" she asked.

There was a burst of laughter, and she turned and smiled as the celebrant repeated the question. "I will," she replied.

The celebrant asked Max the same question. He didn't hesitate. "I will." And his eyes never left hers. Laura didn't hear the last few words of the celebrant. But she saw their effect in Max's face. He was smiling as he stepped toward her and pressed those magical lips to hers.

The warmth of his mouth against hers, his breath against her skin, caused that now familiar flip of the stomach. There was a pause when he was about to pull away but he hesitated and, taking advantage of his hesitation, she pulled her hands from his and threaded her fingers through his hair, keeping his face against hers. She felt the slight chuckle against her mouth but he didn't pull away. Instead, the kiss deepened and he smoothed his hands around her waist, holding her in place, as much as she was holding him.

The laughter and cheering of the crowd receded and she was aware only of the hum of desire that filled her body, as she focused on the movement of his lips, caressing hers, and the light touch of his tongue slipping along the groove between her lips. She opened her lips to allow entrance to his tongue and groaned as it came into contact with hers. Briefly she pressed against his chest—her breasts squashed against his smooth tuxedo—before she felt a change in him. He squeezed her waist and pulled away with a smile.

"That was some kiss, Mrs. Connelly," he murmured against her mouth.

The spell was broken and she widened her eyes at her new name. *Mrs. Connelly!* She hadn't thought this far ahead, hadn't considered how she'd feel at the loss of her own name, and the acquisition of another. A stranger's name. Now her name.

She stepped back, stunned. His smile faded and he caught her hand in his, threaded his fingers through hers and gripped her hand and propelled her forward. She was saved from embarrassment by the confetti which rained down on them. She spat out some that fell into her mouth and sheltered her eyes from it with her hands, laughing.

"Come on," Max said. "Let's get out of here."

She took a couple of steps and then faltered on her high heels. She bent down, slipped off her shoes and, with them in her hand, walked laughing through the crowds with Max holding her hand tightly, as if making sure she was real, making sure she was going to stay by his side.

But she wasn't. Was she?

THE AFTERNOON HAD BEEN FUN, reflected Laura, as she leaned against the pillar in the reception room, looking at the after-party debris. It had gone on all afternoon and into the evening. Now, most people had left. Max had gone outside to see off his friends. Only a couple of his siblings had been able to make it to the wedding at such short notice and they'd already retired for the night.

"It's customary not to be the last guest standing at your own wedding reception."

Laura looked around to find Kelly standing behind her, two drinks in her hand. She offered her one and Laura took a sip. "It's customary to marry for love, or duty, or anything except a challenge. I don't do customary."

Max turned around, catching the tail end of their conversation. "What's customary?"

"Not me," said Laura, still unable to look at him without her heart quickening.

"I was just saying," said Kelly firmly. "That it's customary not to be the last guest standing at your own wedding reception."

"True." Max grinned at Laura. "It's also customary to look as if you're about to enjoy your honeymoon, that it's not something to feared and endured."

Laura snorted with derision and looked away, not wanting him to see the accuracy of his comment. She hadn't looked further than the wedding ceremony. What came next? Would Max expect to go to bed with her? Laura could have kicked herself. For all the preparatory talks about marketing, about promoting their challenge, they'd never once discussed the personal. It had all been about business.

Kelly and Max exchanged glances.

"Take her away, Max," said Kelly.

Laura shot Kelly a dirty look.

"What?" asked Kelly. "You've a full day tomorrow. You need to get your beauty sleep."

Was that all Kelly had meant? Laura looked at Max who was watching her with an inscrutable look on his face. She had no idea what he was thinking or what he anticipated doing. She just hoped it didn't include kissing because she didn't think her defenses could withstand any more. Just the thought of his kisses made her go weak at the knees.

"Sure." She narrowed her eyes. "So…" She hesitated, unwilling to reveal just how little she knew about what lay in store for her. "Where am I sleeping? Back in my own room?"

"No," said Kelly. "Babe, you're sleeping with Max. Otherwise, it's hardly a challenge completed, is it?"

Laura's face must have betrayed her concern because Max looked uncomfortable while Kelly approached her with a sympathetic look on her face.

"Don't look like that!" said Kelly. "It's just a formality. The room has two double beds in it."

Max put his head to one side and thrust his hands in his pockets. "We're only sharing a room, Laura, that's all."

She picked up her shoes and flicked hair off her face with a look of what she hoped was confidence. "Of course. I didn't think you meant anything different." She walked past him and paused at the door. "Night then, Kelly."

"Night, Laura."

Laura didn't look around, but opened the door. There were a few die-hard photographers sitting around who immediately jumped up and snapped a few photos.

"The two of you together, Laura!" shouted one of them.

"Sure." She looked at Max who put his arm around her and they smiled for the camera.

"Thanks, and goodnight," said Max firmly, as he led Laura away down a passageway to the outside. He opened the back door and they stepped out into the cool of the night. The stars were bright, the air crisp and all around was silent. Laura took a deep breath of air and sighed heavily.

"That was some day."

"Yeah. It's not every day you get married." He took her hand. "This way." He took her around the rear of the building to avoid any more photographers. "I don't know how you cope with this sort of attention all the time."

"I hardly notice it now." They stopped outside their room and she looked up at the dark night, the stars vivid above them. "In fact, I don't think I can live without it. It always seems so… quiet, so lonely, really, when everyone's gone and I'm alone again." A shiver tracked down her spine, and she looked around seeking light, looking for some sign of life amid the darkness. Her eyes settled on the antique lantern, unlit by the front door. "You should get that old lantern fixed."

"It's not necessary," said Max.

She shrugged. "Maybe not, but it would look nice—like a guiding light in the darkness."

He didn't say anything immediately, but when she felt the touch of his finger against her cheek, she looked around, compelled by the blast of lust his touch ignited inside her. "A light to make you feel less alone?"

She nodded.

"You're not alone tonight." He pressed his finger to her lips. "And before you say anything, we can be very chaste… if you want to be."

"I do," she said, even as she reached up on tiptoe, unable to deny the lure of his mouth, the idea of his lips on hers, unable to prevent herself from kissing him.

His hand thrust through her hair as the kiss deepened briefly before they pulled apart, their breathing coming faster now. He grabbed her hand and pulled her into the room. He closed the door behind them and put his arms around her and kissed her senseless once more. He cupped her face in his hands. "You, Laura, are one gorgeous woman." He shook his head in disbelief. "I can't believe we're married." He huffed a brief laugh.

But Laura didn't laugh. It was as if someone had poured

icy cold water over her, effectively extinguishing the heat of her arousal. She gave a small gasp and he dropped his hands. She stepped away and turned to look at the room. "It's a beautiful room," she said, too brightly, walking over to the beds, both covered in matching luxurious pale mohair throws. Everything was pale—white on pale gold, on pewter, on grey. The stone floor was heated and the rugs completed the understated luxury.

"It should be. It's the honeymoon suite."

If she'd needed any more bringing back to reality, that did it. She walked over to the chair by the window, wanting to put distance between them. She flicked the blinds open until she could see the stars. "I could look at these forever." She grimaced to herself, listening to hear what he'd do.

He kicked off his shoes and jumped on the bed. Her heart sank and butterflies danced in her stomach.

"Come to bed," said Max.

Laura turned to see him stretched out on the bed, still dressed, but with his bow tie unraveled and his white shirt open.

"I'm not tired," said Laura between gritted teeth, as she continued to peep through the blinds.

"What are you looking at, Mrs. Connelly?"

She glared at him. "Mrs. Connelly indeed! I didn't imagine for one minute that I wouldn't come out of this thing as Ms. McKinney."

"Don't look at me. I left it in the hands of Chelsey."

"And I left it in the hands of Kelly. I thought she'd have known better."

He shook his head. "Come here...Laura."

She looked at him and frowned. She didn't want to get close to him, she didn't want him to see how weirdly upset she felt.

He cocked his head to one side and sighed. "Okay." He got

off the bed and went to the smaller bed. "This is where I'll sleep. *Now* will you go to bed?"

She rubbed her chilled arms. "It's cold at night, now, isn't it?"

His eyes softened and he walked up to her. "Only if you stand in front of an open window at three in the morning."

He reached out and she held her breath. Part of her—a larger part than she'd imagined—felt a thrill run through her at the thought he might touch her, might kiss her like he had before. That part was disappointed when he reached around her and closed the window.

"Now, Laura, don't be startled, but I'm going to give you a hug."

She stepped away. "I don't need a hug."

"I think you do. You look like someone who's about to step up to their execution. Anyone would think you'd never been alone in a man's bedroom before."

She tried to prevent the heat creeping up to her cheeks. She looked away and walked toward the bathroom, hoping he wouldn't see her embarrassment, hoping he wouldn't continue with that conversation, hoping he would stop trying to understand her. She didn't *want* to be understood, least of all by a man she was completely alone with. Least of all by a man who threatened to penetrate the defenses she'd spent the last five years very successfully erecting. They'd been strong, withholding numerous assaults —until now.

She shut the door and fell back against it, closing her burning eyes.

MAX DIDN'T BOTHER UNDRESSING. He turned out all the lights, leaving only a dim light beside the bed and lay on his bed and listened to Laura turn on the shower. She was an enigma.

He'd thought her so easy and straightforward when he'd first met her. It turned out she was anything but.

When she opened the door, a waft of fragrant steam emerged from the bathroom and for a moment she was framed by light—her hair wet from the shower, all traces of the 'hairdo' gone. She was wearing a robe which was tightly sashed around her waist. She walked over to the bed, climbed in and turned out the dim sidelight.

He waited to see if she'd say anything. But she didn't. There wasn't even any sound of activity from the lodge, nor any nocturnal animals, or people, to alleviate the heavy, pregnant silence. Seemed everyone and everything was dead to the world after the long day. Everyone, except them. He let his heart beat once, twice, three times, before he spoke.

"How come you've never slept with anyone, Laura?"

He heard her shift suddenly in the bed.

"How did you know? I thought…" He could almost hear her bite her lip, not wanting to continue.

"You thought that your secret was hidden under your flirtatious ways. You thought that all the while you dressed the total opposite of a Puritan, people wouldn't discover your secret."

She didn't say anything and he wondered if he'd pushed her too far. But there was no going back now.

"It's not a hanging offense, you know. Being…inexperienced," Max continued.

"Of course it's not. I know that." He heard her toss the covers to one side and sit on the edge of the bed. "It's simply because I don't want to be discussed like that. So it seemed easier to appear… one way… the experienced way, so I didn't have to talk about it, defend it, promote it. *Anything* it. It's just me. It's who I am."

"Fair enough. It's your personal life. Not for them, or me, to talk about."

"Yes, but I don't have a personal life, do I?" She sounded closer now. She must have turned to face him. Not that he could see her in the heavy darkness.

"And isn't that what you wanted? Isn't that something you've been running from?" He paused but she made no answer. "Maybe I'm wrong. Maybe there's some other reason you're inexperienced."

"I'm a virgin, Max. Not simply inexperienced. I have zero experience with men, despite how it seems, despite how I come across."

"Why? Sorry, but I'm curious."

He could picture her shrugging. "It wasn't something I ever wanted to do."

"Why not? From the way you kiss, I know you're warm and into men. But you've really not slept with anyone? You're what, twenty-two, you said?"

She gave a small grunt of assent. Then she cleared her throat. "Contrary to the way men think, women don't all want to jump into bed with them. My mom always said I'd know when the time was right. And it hasn't been right... yet."

He lay on the bed, his hands behind his head and considered her reply. "Fair enough. For anyone else. But you?" He shifted on his side so he could face her in the darkness. "You push yourself constantly beyond your comfort zone. You do this on every point except this one thing?"

"That's different. That's emotional. That's inside me. I can't risk that."

Her voice had changed, had become quieter, more vulnerable. It got to him. He could never bear seeing anything or anyone hurting without trying to help them.

"Laura."

"Yes." Her voice was husky as if she was trying to stop herself from crying.

"I have a really big bed. And if you came over here, I'd put out my arm and you could lie down beside me."

He heard a short intake of breath. "What then?"

"You could put your head on my chest, and I could stroke your hair."

"Really? Is that all?"

"Sure."

"But why would you want to do that?"

"Because you're scared and I hate seeing anybody or anything scared. Because I want to comfort you, to quiet your fears and make you feel better."

The silence of the night seemed to thicken. He felt rather than heard her stand and walk to his bed. He was still lying on top of the bed and she sat down, swung her legs onto the bed and laid her head on his chest.

He nearly laughed at the simplicity of the action. In the dark he could almost imagine someone else, other than Laura, had come to him. Her actions bore no resemblance to the woman he'd come to know, come to like—a lot—over the past few weeks. But, as he moved his head closer to hers, he smelled her lemony scent—a combination of shower gel, shampoo and the remains of her perfume, and knew it was her. He let his hand fall gently on her head and drew his fingers down her damp hair, shifting it from her face.

She sighed, her breath warm against his chest, and he smiled to himself. He lay silent, looking up to the ceiling, watching the rise of the moon cast its light into the previously dark room. It lit Laura's blonde hair, making it gleam dully like forgotten pewter. And, with each stroke of her hair, he felt something shift inside of him. He pressed his lips together tightly, unwilling to acknowledge what was happening to him. He never felt emotional. Never. That was for his sisters. That was for his over-emotional father. It wasn't for him.

He heard her breathing change as she relaxed and fell into much-needed sleep. He heard it because he couldn't fall asleep so easily. Her vulnerability caught at the heart of him. And he didn't want that. And, for the first time, he wondered whether this challenge, which they'd both taken on so lightly, was such a good thing—especially for her.

7

"SURELY THE BRIDEGROOM'S FAMILY DOESN'T DISAPPROVE OF OUR LOVELY LAURA?" @TELLTALEGIRL #HAPPYFAMILIES

"*L*aura." Her name briefly penetrated her sleep before fading away. "Laura." Her name was called again, but not in the angry way her father used. This was softly spoken and persuasive in a way which didn't break into her dreams so much as become a part of them. Dreams of her childhood home—the place where she'd gotten her beloved puppy and had run riot through the orchards in the long twilight evenings. She could even smell the orange blossom that filled the air in spring.

"Laura." There it was again. Except this time, she felt the soft tickle of something against her cheek. She wrinkled her nose and tried to brush it away, but it wouldn't go. She blinked her eyes open and was immediately faced with a pair of smiling tawny eyes.

"For someone who doesn't sleep much, you sure slept well last night."

"Max!" She sat up groggily and found that she was still dressed in the robe. But now she had a duvet snugly tucked around her.

He picked up a tray of coffee and croissants from which a

stomach-teasing aroma arose. "Here. I thought you might be hungry."

He placed the tray on her lap and she took a bite of the still-warm croissant. "Have you eaten?" she said, spooning some orange marmalade onto the plate.

"Yes. I've been out." He gestured outside. "There's a fair bit of interest already."

Laura frowned. "What time is it?"

"Ten."

Her eyes widened and she pushed the tray aside and jumped out of bed, picking up her phone to check the time. "It can't be. I never sleep more than five hours. Never. It's unheard of. It's—"

"Ten," he repeated. "You slept seven hours straight."

She shook her head. "But that's impossible." She screwed up her eyes at the phone then looked up at him. "It's ten."

"That's what I said," said Max, grinning as he picked up one of her croissants and took a bite. "You slept like a baby."

She glanced at the bed. "Were you in the bed the whole time?"

"For a while but, after a few hours, I left. You were sleeping so deeply I was afraid to move in case I disturbed you. So I slept over there." He indicated the other bed. Sure enough, the bed had a rumpled duvet and a pillow with an indented head shape.

"Oh!" She pulled her robe belt tighter, suddenly shy. He looked away. "I'll go next door to the sitting room and give you some space. Then, when you're ready, we'll face your adoring public together."

She was grateful. She usually wasn't shy physically but here, now, with this man, she most definitely was. "Thanks." She looked inside the wardrobe. "Kelly's thought of every-thing. Even has my clothes hanging in here." It felt strange that Kelly had thought of today when she hadn't. Seems like

Kelly had a better handle on her life than she had. She scooped up some undies off the shelf and grabbed the closest jeans and top and clutched them to her as if they'd protect her from her new husband.

"Max."

"Yes?" He turned around with a smile.

"About last night."

"Yes," he said slowly. "What about it?"

"We didn't have sex."

"I noticed."

"You… won't tell anyone, will you?"

He frowned. "Of course not. That's personal between you and me."

She smiled, relieved. "Yes. And"—she shrugged—"you know, while I'm open about practically everything in my life, I'd prefer not to answer questions about my sex life."

"Or lack of it."

"Precisely." She sighed. "It's just I don't want to have to talk about all that stuff."

"Of course. It's personal."

"Precisely."

"That's two 'preciselys' in one morning." He grinned. "I'm on a roll. Now, how about you go shower and we get out of here. Kelly wants to see you as soon as possible."

"Sure."

"Plus the fact your fans have discovered which room you're in. They're over the back fence. Sounds like they're agitating to see you."

Laura pulled aside the curtain and looked out. Brilliant sunshine streamed through the window at the same time her name was called out in an excited chorus. Teenage heads bobbed up over the far fence. She waved, instantly relaxing— she was back on familiar territory.

~

"LAURA!" said Kelly excitedly. "You won't believe it. You know that gig we were trying to get in Russia? Well, they contacted us! And the offers of product endorsements are rolling in."

"Oh," said Laura walking to the sideboard and picking up an apple. She tossed it in the air, caught it and took a bite.

"Is that all you can say?"

Laura mumbled and pointed to her full mouth.

"What?"

Laura swallowed. "If it keeps you happy, then that's fine." She sat down. "Any news about the next challenge?"

"You have a number lined up." Kelly's frown deepened as she scanned through the list of them. "But—"

"But what?"

"Most of them are about getting you and Max together."

"What's wrong with that? After all, we are married."

Kelly grimaced. "I don't know. It looks like everyone's gunning to have you guys alone. Alone and, well, kissing."

It was Laura's turn to frown. "Give me that!" She twisted the laptop around and scanned the list. "These aren't the usual challenges. They're, they're..." For once Laura was stumped for words.

"Sexy. Everyone is intrigued by your relationship with Max. People are speculating on Twitter about what happened last night."

Laura blushed as she read through some of the tweets. "I didn't expect stuff like this." She nibbled her lip. "What the hell have I done, Kelly? People are more interested in my sex life than my challenges now." She sat down heavily and gazed into the mid distance as images of her future played out in her mind, like a film with an unexpectedly depressing ending. "I've really stuffed up this time."

Kelly placed a hand on Laura's shoulder. The silence before Kelly spoke told Laura volumes. Things *had* changed and they both knew it. The course of their lives, of their challenges, had taken a U-turn when she'd married Max.

"Come on," Kelly said. "It's not that bad."

Laura looked up mournfully. "Say it again, like you mean it."

"I do. Max is a great guy." Kelly scrolled down the page. "And anyway, see, here! It's Telltale Girl. She doesn't mention your sex life once."

Laura peered at the screen. "No," she replied gloomily. "She wants to know when I'm going to be invited home to meet Max's family and wonders why his father didn't attend the wedding." She looked up at Kelly. "So what? My father didn't attend either."

"So everything! Telltale Girl's tweets are too influential to be dismissed easily."

There was a knock at the door and Chelsey poked her head around. "Okay if Max and I come in? I thought it would be a good idea to have a debrief on how the marriage is going so far."

"Sure."

Chelsey took a seat next to Kelly while Max smiled at Laura and stood a little distance away, leaning against the wall, as if he really didn't want to be there. Laura could sympathize with that feeling.

Chelsey handed a list to Kelly who reciprocated. Kelly let out a low whistle. "This is looking better than we could have imagined."

"Laura, these product endorsements which include both you and Max will mean you can put your feet up for the rest of your life," said Kelly.

Laura grunted. "Why would I want to do that?"

Kelly let out an exasperated sigh. "It's a figure of speech."

She waved the spreadsheets at her. "This means that you don't have to worry about anything ever again. You can go *where* you like and do *what* you like."

"I do that now."

"Then why the hell did you agree to get married?"

Chelsey and Max exchanged glances. Max pushed himself leisurely from the wall and came and stood in front of Laura. "Same reason I did, I guess. It was a challenge, something new, something fun… and it'll be good for business."

Laura appreciated Max jumping to her defense.

"And it's definitely going to set Max and this lodge up for the future," said Chelsey. "He's received offers of product endorsements, and bookings for next year from all over the world." She looked up at Max. "It's gold, Max. Pure gold." She glanced at Laura. "So long as you keep it up. So long as this thing doesn't disintegrate before it's had a chance to gain momentum."

"What are you saying, Chelsey?" asked Laura.

"I'm saying that you and Max need to pay attention to Telltale Girl and others saying the same thing." Chelsey looked up from the laptop where she'd been reading through the latest from Laura's top blogger. "Seems Telltale Girl noticed that your father refused to come to the wedding."

"Who the hell is this Telltale Girl, anyway?" asked Max.

"If I knew that I'd have called her by her name," said Chelsey. "Any idea, Kelly?"

Kelly shrugged. "It doesn't matter who she is, all that's important is to know that she's influential. She noticed Max's father wasn't at the wedding and you don't have to be Einstein to work out he's not best pleased with the marriage. And, if she starts off a rumor that Laura isn't welcome into your family then the bad publicity will snowball and everyone's business will suffer."

"And you don't want that, do you?" asked Chelsey. "You

guys have got to keep this together for the required time if you're to win the challenge, if all these offers, endorsements, bookings, and business propositions aren't to vanish in a puff of smoke." She turned to Max. "You've got to make it work Max. That is, unless you're no longer interested in what this can do for your business?"

The provocative question hung in the air. Laura looked into Max's searching gaze. He was silently asking her the same question. After last night, when her inner vulnerability had been revealed to him, he knew how uncomfortable she was feeling about everything and he was giving her the opportunity to call the whole thing off.

"Max?" asked Chelsey, her manicured fingernails tapping lightly on the desk. "Your silence suggests you're having second thoughts. Do you really want to turn your back on a future like this, after all our hard work?"

"Laura? Over to you," said Max.

Laura swallowed as conflicting thoughts ran through her head. If she did, what then? Would all of this attention disappear? She sighed. Of course it wouldn't. She'd opened a Pandora's box and there was nothing either she or Max could do to close it until it had run its course. She shook her head. "No. Let's continue. It's too late to do anything else."

"Okay." He nodded to Chelsey. "Let's get on with it."

"Good." Chelsey resumed her tapping on the keyboard.

Laura jumped up from her chair. "I'm okay with everything. I'll catch you all later." She had to get out of there. Breathe some fresh air, give herself the illusion that she still had some freedom.

KELLY AND CHELSEY EXCHANGED LOOKS.

Kelly rose. "I'll go join her. Just make sure things stay on track. I'll leave you to organize Max."

Max watched Kelly go before turning to Chelsey. "What, am I some errant child who needs organizing now?"

"Kelly's words, not mine, Max. But you do employ me to organize, so let's get this sorted here and now."

He swore under his breath. "This is more complicated than I thought it would be."

"It's all fine. You just have to play along for a few months and, honestly, don't tell me you don't like Laura, because I know you do. How hard can it be to hang out with her for a few months?"

"It's easy hanging out with Laura. She's great. But it's all the rest of it. The expectations, the invasion of privacy."

"Let's just get on with it. We'll try to organize you some private time, we'll schedule some down time for you both."

He grunted. "Schedule! Organize! I used to be able to disappear into the bush with my mates for weeks at a time, whenever I felt like it."

"That was before you decided to expand." She wrinkled her brow. "This isn't like you. What's up?"

"It's Laura. She doesn't look happy about this now."

"Then she should have thought about it before. She'll have to suck it up. You know she's tough. She'll do it. It's just new to her."

"New to me, too," he muttered.

"That's why we need a plan. And let's start off with Telltale Girl's comments. They're enough to cast doubt on the marriage, and the business. You need to persuade Telltale Girl that this challenge is being taken seriously. And that means dealing with your father's disapproval."

Max huffed. "That's ridiculous! Why should my father's disapproval stop people coming here?"

"Because everyone loves Laura and everyone hates on people who *don't* love Laura."

"I don't hate Laura."

"No, but you're tainted by your father's opinions. You need to get him on side."

"You've met my father, you know what he's like."

"He's charming."

"Your idea of charm is different to mine. He's stubborn, he's opinionated, he's—"

"He's also still handsome, in that Paul Newman kind of way, and he's charismatic—a lot like his eldest son."

Max looked up at her. "You think I'm charismatic?"

"I *know* you are. Fortunately after you dumped me for a string of other women I've found myself immune to your charisma."

"I didn't dump you. I simply..." Max couldn't find the right words.

She sighed and took pity on him. "You simply finished the relationship. I know. You were too honest to continue with something you didn't mean. But it still felt like I'd been dumped. Unceremoniously."

"I didn't realize we were in deep enough for ceremony."

"No." She shot him a dirty look. "You didn't." Then a slow smile spread over her face. "But you're sure into ceremony, now."

It was Max's turn to frown. Both he and Laura had known what they were letting themselves in for and neither were into marriage so it had no meaning. But still... there had been something missing at the wedding and afterwards. Nothing that anyone would have noticed. Everyone had a good time. The event was a success by every measure. But he couldn't get the image out of his brain of Laura, standing alone at the end of the deck, looking out across the mountains, her shoes in her hands. There had been something so deeply sad about it. He didn't know if it had been in the set of her shoulders, something tense and afraid, or in the beauty of the image, alone on her wedding day, surrounded by flowers and the majestic mountains.

And then, later, at night when Laura had appeared so innocent, so vulnerable, the image had come to him and remained. At the time he'd thought his reaction had been a figment of his imagination, but it was only later he realized it was real. Laura was holding something back. She pretended to share her life with the rest of the world. But she didn't. There was something too important for her to share. And it was this which had caught somewhere deep inside. Plucked a string which had vibrated, stirring things he didn't know he could feel.

"I'll tell Dad we're coming."

"When?"

"This weekend."

THE CHOPPER LANDED in the neighboring paddock—the closest flat land to Belendroit—and Max slid back the door.

Laura jumped out. Head bent, she walked quickly away from the chopper and looked around.

As Max slid back the door and signaled to the pilot, the helicopter noise increased and dust whirled all around. The helicopter took off and flew out across the harbor, back toward Christchurch.

"Welcome to Akaroa."

"You've been spoiled, Max. First Queenstown and now this?" With a sweep of her hand she indicated the harbor, ringed by hills, picture-perfect under the morning sun.

"True enough."

"It's gorgeous. The light feels different here. Softer, gentler. And listen." She stood stock still in the road and turned around.

"What?"

"There's nothing. Total silence." She laughed. "No one staring at us... wondering."

"About our nights together." Nights, he reflected, which had continued as the first night. No kisses—he sensed that neither of them dared to kiss as before for fear of real intimacy. Nights in which Laura slept well, while he lay awake watching her, thinking about his life, about his family, about his mother who he knew wouldn't have approved of the situation he'd found himself in. She'd have approved of Laura—his mother loved nothing more than someone who was full of life and fun—but she definitely wouldn't have approved of his "arranged" marriage.

"Yeah. I never used to mind speculation but it's harder now it's so personal."

"It's only for a few months. And then we can return to our worlds."

"Do you think they'll ever be the same again?"

He shrugged, knowing what she wanted to hear. But he couldn't reassure because he didn't lie. "No. Nothing's ever the same. Everything changes and we change with it." He saw her face fall and wanted to see her smile again. "But it's not always for the worst. Who knows? I may make you a better person."

She grinned and thumped him. "You're impossibly conceited, Max Connelly."

He heard a shout, followed by the barking of dogs, and they both looked down the hill to where a man stood on the road beside an open gate. Beside him were two cocker spaniels looking around short-sightedly, barking in response to their master's call. They knew something was up, even if they had no idea what. Behind his father, a house sat nestled amidst sheltering trees from which a lawn ran down to a secluded beach.

Laura gave a low whistle. "Is that your family's place?"

"Yep. Welcome to Belendroit. And that's my father and our two mad dogs, Stanley and Boo. Let's get this over with."

"Dad!" Max said as they reached the road. He noticed his father hadn't moved. He still stood, hands casually thrust in his pockets, in a 1970s pose, his face without its usual affable smile. But the dogs ran up to him, wagging their tails, jumping and running around in circles, barking. Max stopped to pet them. "Dad, this is Laura McKinney." He turned to her. "Laura, this is my father, Jim Connelly."

Laura stuck out her hand. "Mr. Connelly, nice to meet you."

Jim's frown hovered over fierce eyes. "Laura McKinney? I thought it was Laura Connelly from what I read in the papers."

Laura glanced at Max. Even the dogs sensed the tension, scuttling behind Jim and sitting expectantly.

"How about a simple 'hello' and 'welcome to Belendroit', Dad? You can do the third degree thing later if you insist."

Jim Connelly's lips firmed into a line. "I'm sorry, son, but I've been stewing about this since I first heard. I could hardly believe it. Not even invited to my eldest son's wedding!"

"You wouldn't have liked it, Dad, it was crazy."

"It would have been nice to have had the opportunity to make up my own mind." He turned to Laura with a constrained smile. "My eldest son has always been a mystery to me. Never wanted to settle down and then suddenly, this! Out of the blue. However, I can understand it a little better now I've met you."

"Come on, Dad! Mum said you proposed on the first date! And were married within the month."

"Things were done differently then, son. We wanted to start a family as soon as possible."

Max snorted. He knew what that meant.

"Do you intend to have a family?" Jim asked Laura.

"Dad! For God's sake. What kind of question is that to ask?"

He turned a benign face to Max. "A reasonable one."

Max felt Laura's touch on his arm. "It's fine, Max." Laura turned to his father. "No, I... *we*... won't be having a family. I don't want to have children."

"Not have children!"

"Dad," warned Max. "It's none of your business."

"Of course it's my business. They would be my grandchildren. Your mother and I had hoped for a rugby team of grandchildren by now." He shook his head at the mention of Max's mother. "She'd turn in her grave if she could have seen this."

Max held up his hand. "Let's stop this now. Apologies, Laura. My father appears to have forgotten his reputation for 'charm'."

Jim grunted and sighed. "You're right, of course. But you must know—" Whatever he was going to say was halted by another arm raise by Max. "Okay." He rocked back on his heels and took a deep intake of air. "Laura," he said with a rush of breath. "I am very pleased to meet you and I apologize for my boorish outburst." As if sensing the change in their master, the dogs leaped around to greet Laura. Their master obviously now approved of their visitor.

The change from fierce—those white bushy brows rose up from his blue eyes like heavy clouds revealing a bright promising day ahead—to charming was instantaneous and disarming. Max sighed to himself. Chelsey was correct. His father *was* charming and, unfortunately, enjoyed the fruits of his charms without regard to consequences. There were times when this had made his mother deeply unhappy and that was something Max would never forgive him for.

Laura wiped her hands, which the dogs had decided to

lick copiously, onto her jeans, and took his extended hand and shook it. "And I apologize for the unusual circumstances."

"Laura, welcome to Belendroit. Please forgive a stick-in-the-mud old man. I've been around too long to understand things like this." He waved his hand abstractly. Max and Laura exchanged glances. "Come on in, and I'll make a pot of tea. Amber was by yesterday and dropped off a cake. Vegan, I'm afraid. And I suspect lentils are involved if the taste is anything to go by. But it's okay when warmed and eaten with a lot of cream and jam."

Laura grinned and fell into step with Jim. "Amber?" she asked, ducking her head to avoid the late-blooming flowers which hung from the overgrown bushes lining the driveway.

"Max's little sister. She's the baby," said Jim, his expression warming. He obviously had a big soft spot for his baby girl, despite her penchant for lentils.

"A twenty-one-year-old baby," said Max, walking on her other side. "Whose love for animals is as strong as her love for people. Stanley and Boo think all their Christmases have come at once when Amber's here. She spoils them rotten." He picked up a ball that was lying on the ground and threw it for the dogs. Laura was pretty sure that Amber wasn't the only Connelly to spoil the dogs.

"Hasn't Max told you about his siblings?" asked Jim.

Laura and Max exchanged a quick glance. "A little. I met Rachel in Wellington before I came to Queenstown. And I met Lizzi at Queenstown Lodge."

"Apart from Amber, there's Rob who lives in London, Gabe who works in Akaroa, and Cameron—he's the proverbial black sheep of the family, we don't hear anything from him from year to year." Jim sighed. "And then there was poor Jonny who died overseas." Jim suddenly looked up at the house, which revealed itself from the grassy drive they'd walked down. He stopped walking and regarded the house. "Belendroit," he said simply.

Laura surveyed the old colonial house, noting the lanterns which jutted out from both sides of the house, as well as either side of the front door. "It has the same type of lantern as your lodge, Max."

"Yeah, well, that's Mum's influence."

"She always liked her home to be welcoming and reckoned lights did just that," said Jim.

"They do," said Laura with a laugh. "In fact, the house looks like it's smiling!"

"You're not the first to say that," said Jim. "It's the way the roof juts out over the first floor windows, like eyebrows raised in surprise. And with the veranda fretwork framing the door—"

"That's the smile," added Max.

"It certainly looks a happy house." She stepped forward. "I've never seen a house with such character before. It looks sweet, like you want to look after it."

"I rather think it's the other way around," said Jim.

Jim's expression turned reflective as he stepped toward the house with Laura by his side. It wasn't like him, thought Max as he fell into step. Maybe this marriage was affecting more people than he'd imagined.

They walked up between the two wings of the house onto the deep veranda, which provided welcome shade from the sun.

"Max, why don't you show Laura around while I go and boil the kettle?"

Max set up the camera. "Let's get some photos of us together first."

Despite Jim's grumblings, the photos were quickly taken before Jim disappeared inside the house.

Max smiled at Laura and gestured to the open French doors which led off the veranda. "Belendroit awaits."

Laura let out a low whistle. "This is like another world. How old is this place?"

"Around 1890 as far as we can make out. It was one of the first houses built in the area by the French settlers."

"French?"

"Yes, the French settled around here. In fact, New Zealand would have been a French colony, if it hadn't been for a couple of very determined English men who set up the New Zealand Company and brought English people by the shipload out here to settle, before the French could organize anything."

"I had no idea."

Max watched as Laura walked into the old-fashioned drawing room and turned around slowly, taking it all in. He tried to imagine it through her eyes—from the overflowing bookcases which flanked the central fireplace, its toffee-colored wood complementing the William Morris wallpapered walls, to the lush, richly colored velvets and silks draped over the back of the leather chesterfield couch which was cracked in places, rubbed smooth with an age-old patina in others. Victorian colors of ruby red, dark green and regal blues were interspersed with the occasional startling magenta. The whole was warm and welcoming, and consistent with the style and age of the homestead and its ramshackle, sprawling character.

She turned to him with bright eyes. "I feel like a child who has stepped into a fairy-tale house full of secrets and treasures, all with stories attached, waiting to be discovered."

He grunted softly. She'd hit the nail on the head. "This place *is* full of stories. My *mother* was full of stories." He joined Laura who was looking at a large book, open on a table placed behind the chesterfield. "Dad's a bit of an anti-quarian. This is a map of the area before the English arrived."

She peered at it. "And we're here?" Her finger hovered over the old paper, not daring to touch it.

"Yes. We existed before Akaroa did. The town began some twenty years after my ancestors built this house. The bay isn't named on the map. But it's always been known in the district as Lantern Bay."

"Because of your family's fixation with lanterns?" ventured Laura.

"Exactly. You can see the lights of the lanterns from miles away."

"That's lovely. You must feel really grounded with such a history. I can't imagine it."

"I guess so, but I feel I belong in Queenstown now. That's where I was happiest growing up. That's where my future is."

"Mine is to keep on moving." She gave a quick bright grin, as if daring him to challenge her statement.

He dared. "You don't find it lonely?"

"Lonely? Are you kidding? I'm never alone."

She was wrong and he was sure she knew it. From the beginning he'd been intrigued by her and now he knew her better—had been given a glimpse of the real, vulnerable Laura—his intrigue had turned to something else. He turned from her abruptly. But what? Surely it was nothing more than the same impulse which made him want to protect his sisters? That was it, he thought to himself. This feeling which Laura stirred was nothing more than a desire to protect—pure and simple.

"Tea!" called Jim from outside. They both looked through the French doors to see him set down a tray on the large table which dominated the veranda. He looked toward them. "You haven't progressed very far! I'll take you around myself after tea and this"—he glanced with distaste at the cake—"lentil creation."

As Laura followed Max outside, she couldn't shrug off the feeling that she'd walked right into a fairy tale. Even outside, the veranda was chock full of character and style. Not in the sense her parents would have used the word "style", but "style" it definitely was.

She sat in a white cane chair, made comfortable with hand-embroidered cushions from another age, and smoothed her hand over the silk stitches. Her parents' house had nothing like this—everything was modern in their Californian home, created by machines. They'd have hated the fact that some of the threads were worn and there was a splash of red—most likely wine, judging from the straw-covered chianti bottles in which candles melted down the side—which would have been reason enough for her mother to have given it to charity. Seems charity began at home here.

Laura sat beside a thick wisteria vine around which glimpses of the bay could be seen. In front of them lay the small thicket of trees which protected them from the road, which, gathering by the lack of traffic, was obviously not often used.

"How do you like your tea, Laura?" asked Jim.

Laura couldn't remember the last time she'd drunk tea, or how she'd drunk it. But she didn't want to come across as rude. "Oh, black, please."

"Excellent. Earl Grey should always be drunk black, with a twist of lemon. Is that how you like it?"

"Yes, please." She did now, anyhow.

Max hadn't sat down, he looked around, uprooting some withered plants. "You should get someone to help you around here, Dad. At least in the garden." He rattled an overgrown vine, part of which had died. "They'd sort this lot out for you."

"I don't need help," his father said firmly.

"You're not getting any younger."

"Thanks for the reminder," Jim said grimly. "Besides, Betty comes in and tidies up a bit."

Max scoffed. "She does a whole lot more than that! She does it surreptitiously so as not to hurt your feelings."

Jim gave Max a warning look from beneath his impressive white eyebrows. "She's a friend."

Laura coughed and lifted her fine-bone china cup, which sat on a mismatched saucer. All the china was a mixture of different English potteries. She took a quick sip. "Um, delicious." And to her surprise, it was.

Jim's expression changed instantly as he turned back to her. "A woman of discernment." He sat back in the cushioned chair which was obviously his usual seat, if the opened books, pairs of glasses and coffee cup, complete with dried remains, was anything to go by. "So, tell me how you two met."

Laura and Max exchanged glances. She had no idea how much Max wanted to tell his father.

"I first saw Laura speeding down the hill by the Lodge on a racing bike, take off from a jump which only the most experienced bikers tackle, land in one piece and stop immediately before the drop down to the road."

Jim's startling eyebrows raised toward his thick snowy hair. "Wonderful!" he exclaimed and thumped his foot on the veranda, making an alarming hollow sound, as if his foot could disappear through the old boards at any moment.

"It was fun," said Laura.

"So you're a mountain biker. My son Jonny used to mountain bike."

"I do a bit of everything."

"And what do you do for a living?"

Again she and Max exchanged looks. "Just that really. A bit of everything." She gave Max some time but he said nothing. If he wasn't going to take the lead, then she'd have to. She took a deep breath. "I accept challenges for a living."

"Really? What kind?"

"Any kind."

"And how does that bring in money?"

"We—that's me and my friend, Kelly, who manages everything—monetize my online presence. Companies pay us to promote their products. But we only do that if we believe in them."

There was a long silence in which Jim steepled his fingers and pressed them to his mouth, his eyes trained on her. She shifted uncomfortably in her seat.

"I guess you think it's a strange way to live, but"—she lifted her chin—"it works for me."

"And marriage to my son was simply another challenge to you?"

If she'd felt uncomfortable before, she wished the beautiful house of Belendroit would sink into the lush vegetation, taking her with it. She nodded and took a hasty sip of scalding tea.

"That's it, Dad," said Max. "Got it in one. A challenge for us both because neither of us are into marriage."

Jim closed his eyes briefly as if he'd been struck. He opened his eyes with a sigh. "I'm glad your mother isn't here to listen to you say such things. It would have upset her."

While the conversation was tense, Laura also found it strangely fascinating. Her own family was uncommunicative and her mother, cold. Little was ever said about anything meaningful. But here, in the Connelly household, it seemed much was said, and much was meant. She followed Jim's gaze to Max who, for the first time, also looked uncomfortable.

"Let's leave Mum out of this."

"Why?" answered Jim.

"Because you have no idea what she would have said. Because all she wanted was the best for all of us. And for you, despite everything."

Laura was now not only fascinated but confused. It seemed there was a subtext to this conversation about which she knew nothing.

"I may have made mistakes—"

Max's scoffing laugh interrupted Jim. "And some!"

"But I loved your mother. Whatever I did or didn't do, we both believed in marriage and, whatever you care to think, we had a very happy one."

Max pushed himself off the wall. "Who are you trying to kid, Dad?"

Jim rose from his chair. Despite his age he was the same height as Max. "You know nothing of marriage, Max, and this... this preposterous marriage of yours only proves that."

Laura felt she was intruding and stood up because it didn't feel right to sit and watch this. "I'm sorry, Jim. We thought this would be a good idea. It obviously isn't. I didn't want to upset you."

It was Jim who turned from Max to look at Laura. "You're a wonderful girl, Laura. A blind man could see that and, it seems, even Max can. But this marriage of yours isn't right. How can it last?"

Laura licked her lips. "It can't, Jim. It won't. That was the nature of the challenge. Marriage for six months, after which it'll be annulled."

Jim pressed his lips together and looked away. His gaze fell to the camera. "That's why you wanted the photo," he said sadly.

"Yes," said Max, picking up the camera, his movements revealing his agitated state. "We needed a photo to show the corporate sponsors that it's a real marriage in the full sense of the word, including family." Max ignored Jim's scoffing noise when he said "real". "Because it's not only Laura who's attracting corporate sponsors, it's me. This marriage will give me invaluable publicity for the Lodge."

Jim nodded and shrugged. "This is beyond me. Why don't we all sit down, finish our tea and then I'll show Laura around the property."

"No," said Max. "We have our photo, you've met Laura, so we may as well go now."

"Max!" remonstrated Laura.

He ignored her. "We've done what we came down to do."

"You can't bring Laura here and not show her the rest of Belendroit. Lantern Bay, the house, the gardens."

There was a pleading in Jim's voice which made Laura look anxiously at Max, willing him to take pity on his father and relent.

"It's our life, Dad. You can't steamroll us like you did Mum."

"And you can't continue to blame me for things you know nothing about, and understand less."

Max walked away. Laura looked from Jim to Max, who walked down the drive and disappeared into the trees.

"I'm sorry, Jim. I'm so sorry. I didn't mean for this to happen."

"Of course not. You don't know Max. But I do." He looked to where Max had last been seen, as if he could see him through the trees. "And he's hurting. And I don't know what to do about it."

Laura accepted his kiss on her cheek and a brief hug, but her mind was elsewhere. On Max. On the man she thought she was getting to know, but who she didn't know at all.

8

"FLUSHED CHEEKS…BRIGHT EYES! COULD THIS MARRIAGE BE THE REAL THING?" @TELLTALEGIRL #COULDTHISBELOVE?

*L*aura didn't think she'd ever had such a quiet flight before.

Max had barely spoken the whole journey from Akaroa back to Queenstown. She suddenly understood the meaning of the words alpha male. The grunts alone were Neanderthal. She resorted to her phone, uploading the photo and catching up with her tweets and Facebook posts. She wasn't used to placating grumpy men. She shot him the occasional glance but he seemed equally absorbed in work.

Except one time she looked up and saw him looking out the window with an expression of wounded perplexity and something clicked. This wasn't a grumpy man, this was a sad one.

Sadness, she could handle. She clicked off her phone decisively. He looked around and his expression immediately changed. The spark in his eyes warmed her. He liked her. He really liked her. Good. That made it easier to do what she had to do.

"You okay?" Max asked.

She leaned her head against the headrest, surveying him.

By his reaction she guessed not many people held his gaze as firmly as she did. "Yeah, I'm okay. Not sure your father is, though. He seemed pretty disappointed with us leaving so soon. And in such a way."

"That's fine with me."

"Come on, whatever your father did, he can't have deserved this."

The look of good humor disappeared. "Leave it, Laura."

She looked away. She should leave it. After all, he was right, it *was* nothing to do with her. But the memory of the old man's face as he turned away from them, back toward Belendroit, haunted her. And the sadness in Max's expression... well that got her at a whole different level, one which, while she wasn't prepared to examine too closely, she *was* prepared to act on. Time to dig in.

"It was great meeting your dad—he's a real character."

Max grunted and looked away. "That's one word for him."

"And what word would you use?"

He pursed his lips briefly. "I couldn't restrict it to one."

"Okay. Spill."

He turned to her. "You really want to know?"

"Yes, or I wouldn't have asked."

"He's a cheating, unfaithful, son-of-a-bitch."

Max's eyes blazed and Laura was shocked by the raw anger she saw in his face. He wasn't only sad, he was furious.

"He cheated on your mom?"

"Yeah, he cheated. And all the while he carried on like they were some perfect couple."

"And your mom was okay with that?"

"She didn't know anything about it until years later."

"How long did the affair go on?"

"Long enough."

"How long?" she repeated, more firmly now.

He shrugged. "A couple of weeks."

"Oh, I see," she said, suddenly getting a better picture of what had happened. "And how long were your parents married?"

"Forty years, give or take."

"And how did you mom find out?"

"*I* told her. She was telling me once about how wonderful my dad was and how I should be nicer to him and I couldn't stand it, so I told her."

"What happened?"

"She was devastated. I've never seen her so shocked. It was like her world had tilted on its axis. And so was Dad when he came in on the scene. I left them to it."

"Did they manage to sort it out?"

He didn't speak immediately. "Of course they did. My mother was a forgiving woman. But…"

"But?"

"A month after that she was diagnosed with cancer that hadn't been present on scans taken six months earlier."

"Ah, so you blame your father for your mother's death?"

He looked at her strangely. "Something like that. Some people believe severe shocks affect the body's hormones and can bring on cancer."

"Really?"

"Yeah. Of course no one knows for sure. But whatever way you look at it, Dad's culpable."

"You don't forgive easily, do you?"

"No. You can't change people, you can only accept them or reject them."

"That's a tough line to take."

"It's life."

"And you reject your father."

"I go see him, I hang out at Belendroit from time to time, when I know the others will be there, but I'm never going to have any quality time with him."

"It was a long time ago, you know, Max. I know he did wrong, but even you say he loved your mother. Maybe he's been punished enough now? Maybe it's time to forgive?"

"Not after what he did."

"How do you know exactly what he did?"

"I saw him and his lover coming out of her cottage down the road in the early hours when I was out camping."

"How old were you?"

He shrugged. "Around ten. What does it matter? What does any of it matter? It's past. It's done. Mum's gone and she suffered. And I'll never forgive him for that."

"What was your mom like?"

"Beautiful, caring, kind, but pretty fierce if any of us got out of line. Above everything else, she was very loving. She'd do anything to keep us all happy. Even be sad herself."

"And that, *there*, is why I don't want to commit and have children. Women always put themselves behind everyone else. It sucks!"

He smiled. "And yet here you are, married."

She gave him a quick sideways glance, pleased to have shifted his focus from his father, to teasing her. "Just don't think I'm sacrificing anything for you."

"I wouldn't want you to." His face suddenly serious. "I'd never want anyone I was involved with to be unhappy, to suppress anything they wanted to do, or be."

She swallowed. "Then... whoever you end up with will be a really lucky woman."

His face softened into a smile. "But it won't be my first wife."

She shook her head, not even knowing if he asked a question or made a statement. "I'll be gone in a few months."

"And how are we going to pass that time?"

She shrugged. "Business, I guess. Appearances, I think

Kelly has some TV lined up. Meetings with potential sponsors."

"And you like doing all of that?"

"God no! I just want to be getting on with the next challenge."

"What is it about you and challenges?"

It was Laura's turn to feel uncomfortable. "Don't go analyzing me."

"So it's okay for you to analyze my relationship with my father, but not for me to try to understand you."

"Exactly."

"Okay. I have a plan. I'll arrange some more challenges. And I bet that I'll understand you better at the end of them."

"Doubt that. I'm inscrutable."

"I'll work you out. You'll see."

"So what are these challenges going to be?"

"You'll find out soon enough."

LAURA KICKED off her shoes and stretched out her legs on the bed. She felt unusually shattered.

"Was Akaroa so strenuous?" asked Kelly.

Laura reflected on Max and his father. "A different kind of strenuous. Or maybe it's just marriage—seems its pretty tiring."

"All that sex, eh?"

Laura narrowed her eyes at Kelly. "You know that's not part of the deal, whatever Telltale Girl might be suggesting."

"Might not be part of, but I thought you might have succumbed to Max's many charms."

"I did not."

"Well, let's keep that between us two. Don't want to ruin the image."

Laura sighed. "We have Telltale Girl to carry on the image. You know? I wish sometimes she'd move on to someone else. Leave me alone."

"Really? Looks to me like she just wants you to be happy."

Laura sighed, suddenly even more tired by this thought. "Why should she care? Anyhow, I can create my own happiness."

"Can you?" asked Kelly pointedly.

"Of course I can. I'm happy when I'm in the middle of a challenge. Talking of which, any new ones?"

"A few which you can do in your sleep. I'll schedule them." She scrolled down the page. "And some funny comments about you and Max. Seems everyone's imagining what you guys are up to behind closed doors."

"They'd be disappointed if they knew the truth. Anything else?" Laura really wanted to move away from her and Max, back to the simplicity of life before marriage.

"Hey! Here's a challenge from someone you know."

"Really?"

Kelly looked up with a grin. "Max!"

Laura jumped up and looked over Kelly's shoulder. "What?" She scanned Max's challenge and turned to Kelly and they both burst out laughing. Then Laura stopped. "Earth, Wind and Fire? Sure thing." She stretched over and typed in her usual smiley face with a thumbs-up to accept the challenge.

In HINDSIGHT, Max regretted that his mother's favorite 1970s soul band had been playing in the background when he'd come up with his challenge. But it had seemed appropriate, given Laura's wish to feel everything the world had to offer. Couldn't get more basic than the elements. So he'd gone with it, and had sent the challenge before he'd had time to think it through. It had required all of Chelsey's persuasiveness and organizational skills to make the first challenge happen. And it had also required a very early start.

By the time they flew from Queenstown to a small airport on the North Island's east coast, the sun was high in the clear blue sky and the helicopter was waiting for them.

"So when are you going to tell me exactly where we're going? Any time soon?" Laura looked around as they left the coastline of the wide bay and flew over the deep teal blue of the Pacific Ocean.

He pointed to a small island from which steam billowed. "Real soon. Now, in fact. We're going to where the Pacific Rim of Fire meets the earth's surface. We're taking the challenge backwards, beginning with fire." Laura followed his gaze across the sweep of white-rimmed coastline, out to sea. There, starkly white against a brilliant blue sky and sea sat an island. But not just any island—a perfectly formed volcanic cone.

"*Te Puia o Whakaari.*"

"*Te Puia?*" repeated Laura.

"The Volcano."

"*o Whakaari?*"

"Dramatic. The Dramatic Volcano, the Maori call it. The Europeans call it a whole lot more prosaic name—White Island."

Laura peered out the window at the island which dominated the vast bay. "White Island," she repeated. "Prosaic, but pretty accurate. The drama bit sounds ominous. But it's cool to see from the air."

"From the air? It's a date with fire, remember. As close as I could get to fire. You might not see flames but you'll feel their effect. No," said Max, looking over her shoulder. "We're not staying in the air; we're landing there." He reached over and grabbed a hard hat and breathing mask. "That's what these are for."

Laura took them from him, examining the rubber mask. It was like something from World War II. "You have to be kidding me! You want me to wear this?" She tried it on and looked at him through the plastic mask.

He grinned. "At least your fans won't recognize you. But no, you only have to wear them if the volcano erupts. The ash sets like cement in your lungs. You'll also need a hard hat."

Laura welcomed the familiar thrill of adrenaline as she slipped off her mask and looked down upon the small circular island. Greenery had managed to grow on one side of the volcanic cone whose razor-like edges thrust a thousand feet into the blue sky. Colonies of gannets inhabited the sides of the cone. But most of the island was like some kind of lunar landscape, daubed with bright yellows and oranges, in the middle of which was a smoking cauldron of a lake.

"How come the crater lake isn't any higher? It looks like it's on the same level as the bay."

"It is. It's an ocean volcano. You're only seeing the top third, the rest is under water."

"The colors are crazy!"

"The result of sulphur."

"I can smell it from here."

"Yeah. We won't stay long. The rotten egg smell isn't the best."

"When did it last erupt?"

"2003. It blew from the main crater and sent its lava into the sea. There was some amazing footage."

"Are you sure it's safe?"

He grinned. "No."

.   .   .

THE HELICOPTER SWUNG AROUND and landed. Max jumped out after Laura, watching her as she twirled around.

"This place is crazy! Like a lunar landscape—it's like the world being made." She looked up at where the steam rose from the central crater. "We're going there?"

"Yep."

Laura grinned. "Cool," she said, turning on her camera.

"Pretty hot, actually."

And it was. As they crunched along the gray landscape, interspersed with vivid shades of yellow and orange, the sun shone relentlessly down, the mud bubbled, and steam roared through cracks in the surface, showering boiling water.

Laura coughed and pulled a face. "My throat stings."

Max also felt the burning, tingling feeling at the back of the throat. "It's the sulphur in the steam. It mixes with saliva and forms acid droplets. Turns your teeth black if you're here long enough."

"Then we won't be," she said determinedly, quickening her pace.

"You can turn back if it's too much."

"No way!"

It wasn't far to the crater lake and when they reached it, they recoiled from the heat, and the acrid taste and smell of sulphur. A film of lime green covered the yellow acid of the lake. Laura edged closer to Max and he could sense her unease despite the bravado. Beads of sweat pearled Laura's forehead and upper lip as she turned the camera on them both. He had an urge to sweep them away with his finger.

She spoke into the camera, with the steaming crater lake as a backdrop, before turning to Max.

"The 'fire' date, Max... so where is it?"

"The fire? It's there alright. You think there'd be all this steam without it?"

"I guess not." She stepped back to get a better shot and

Max grabbed and steadied her, his fingers pushing up under her shirt, along the bare skin of her forearm.

"You have to watch your step. You can easily get burned here."

"Burned..." She swallowed. "But no sign of fire."

"You can't always see the danger, or feel the heat, Laura, but you sure can feel its effect. It's there, beneath the surface, burning deep and steady."

She kept filming but had somehow forgotten to speak. He could see her thoughts were moving the same way as his by the flare of desire in her eyes, and the way her gaze dropped to his mouth. What was it about this woman which stirred his feelings like no one before? He had no idea, and no ability to control what he was about to do. He took hold of her hand and tugged her to him and turned the camera off.

"Hey! What are you doing?"

"We're on the top of a volcano, alone, except for the millions of people at the other end of the camera. I didn't want them watching when I did this."

She smiled. "What?"

He bowed his head and kissed her, long and slow, just as he'd been wanting to do since they married. Here, far from any bed, or soft grass, any setting remotely conducive to making love, they were safe from temptation and he reckoned he could indulge himself. When he pulled away he was satisfied to see her eyes still closed, her mouth still partly open. It took all his willpower not to press his lips once more to those soft and receptive lips. "That."

"Ah, that," she said opening her eyes, and touching her lips where his mouth had just swept hers. Suddenly the wind changed direction and a cloud of steam showered its now cool droplets all over them.

"Come on," said Max. "Let's get out of here."

They walked quickly toward the sea, past the erupting earth, pausing briefly beside the old ruins.

"I can't believe people actually lived here. It's so… alien."

"Some of the workers lived here for up to eight years, only going home at Christmas. It was rough. They had to keep cleaning their teeth, as they'd go black and decalcify. In the end an eruption killed them all."

Laura turned away suddenly but not before Max glimpsed a look of shock, which reverberated deep inside him. "Are you okay?"

She brushed the back of her hand across her forehead. "I guess." She shrugged and looked around, her hand reaching for the silver locket she always wore. "This place, the idea of being trapped here, gives me the creeps."

"I didn't think anything spooked you."

He followed her gaze around the steaming center of the island, the yellow, orange and dun-colored ground, and the ruins of the buildings and jetty which stuck out into the blue sea as if trying to escape.

"Nothing much does. But this does." Despite the heat, she shivered.

"Why?" He asked the question lightly but he really wanted to know the answer.

She closed her eyes as if trying to understand her feelings, as if trying to make a shape or a form from the swirl of feelings he could see she was overwhelmed by.

"Because I can't see it."

He chucked under her chin. "You might if you open your eyes," he said with a smile.

She opened them and her expression was deadly serious. His smile dropped.

"The fire, I mean," said Laura. "There are no flames, nothing I can deal with. It's hidden. Like a time bomb waiting to go off. An unstable time bomb which you can't control, but is inescapable. It terrifies me."

Before he could pull her into his arms to try to wipe away that look of fear she turned and walked toward the jetty. Looked like she was going to sit out the wait for the helicopter on the end of the old jetty, as far away from this island as possible.

While Max phoned the helicopter pilot, he watched Laura and thought that, rather than learning more about her, he'd simply discovered there was a whole lot more to her than he'd realized. And also he'd plumbed depths of his own feelings he hadn't known to exist. The more he knew about her, the more he needed to know, the more he needed to grapple with his own feelings for her.

Maybe his next challenge would help him there. He'd ticked off 'fire', that left earth and wind.

THE NEXT CHALLENGE didn't happen until a week later, to allow for Laura's sponsorship commitments. He hadn't seen her as she did a whistle-stop tour of Queensland, which was just as well as, since the wedding, the demand for the Lodge's facilities and for his own appearances had multiplied exponentially.

Chelsey and Kelly's plans for both their businesses was succeeding beyond everyone's wildest imagination. They were happy and Max was pleased with the effect on the Lodge. But he was less pleased to find he couldn't stop thinking about the woman who'd be leaving his life for good in a few short months. Physically, she stirred him, mentally, she engaged him, and emotionally, she intrigued him. To be stirred, engaged and intrigued all at once was something which had never happened before. And he wasn't sure he liked it. Particularly if it wasn't reciprocated. And he had no idea what Laura felt toward him. But he was determined, as well as discovering more about what lay at the heart of her, to find out what her feelings, if any, were toward him.

"I DECIDED to leave the wind until last. It's earth today. We're going caving."

Laura swallowed. How come Max knew what buttons to press, which things she least liked? She'd been down caves before but had never enjoyed it. But she wasn't about to tell anyone that. In her experience if she admitted to a fear, it usually made it worse.

"So what is it with your choice of challenge—Earth, Wind and Fire?"

"I was brought up listening to 1970s soul music. Earth, Wind and Fire was my mum's favorite band."

"I don't think I've ever heard them."

"Your education has been sorely lacking. I'll remedy that as soon as we get back to the Lodge. In the meantime"—he opened the door of the four-wheel drive—"let's get going."

"WE'RE NOT ALONE on this one, then," she said, indicating the two guides who were walking ahead of them through the underground passage.

"No. I'm no expert. I've been caving a few times, but you don't muck about with caves. There's water down there and not much room to maneuver.

She swallowed. "When you say not much room to maneuver, how much exactly?"

He considered. "Well, there are a couple of places where

we'll have to take our helmets off in order to pass through."

Nausea washed through her. She turned away so that he wouldn't see the flush in her cheeks. Take their hats off? How damn small was this place?

"It's fine though, really," continued Max. "Once you're inside the cathedral cave it makes it all worthwhile."

"Okay," she said loudly, trying to convince herself. "That sounds great. Let's get going, shall we?"

Adrenaline spurred her on. She kept moving, not daring to stop in case she had a chance to reflect on how many hundreds of meters of rock and earth were above her. She wriggled along the ground on her stomach, following the person ahead of her, took off her hat when she was told to, passed it to someone and wriggled through, all the time thinking, *I'm going to have to do this again*.

Sheer grit and determination kept her moving forward. It was only when she felt a change in the air, could hear the sound of running water, that she relaxed. Suddenly they emerged into a huge cavern whose top she couldn't see and her fears were forgotten. The guides moved their torches around the space, highlighting dripping orange stalactites, and stone the color of marble, steel and pale gold.

Max stepped up beside her. "What do you think?"

"It's amazing! I've never seen anything like it." She flashed her light up high. "I can't even see the top."

"It's hundreds of feet high. It's part of a huge underground network, only part of which has been explored. It's not open to the public. It's too risky."

"*Now* you tell me." She was only partly joking.

"You're not worried, are you?"

Before she could respond, one of the guides shouted something to Max.

He turned to her with a grin. "Lights out."

"What?"

"We're turning our lights out to get the full impact of this place."

He leaned over and switched hers out, then his, as the guides did the same with all of their light sources. From a place of wonder, the cavern turned into a place of fear. Nothing but blackness, silent except for the water, and its cool damp rising to chill her even further.

Laura cried out. She couldn't help it, wasn't even aware of it, as Max's hand gripped her arm.

"It's okay," he said through the darkness. He pulled her to him, and switched their lights on. He called to the others who did the same. "It's okay. Everything's fine. It's just a trick they do, to show people just how dark it is down here."

She couldn't stop shaking and allowed herself to be folded into Max's arms, needing his warmth and reassurance. She couldn't have said how long she stayed that way but eventually Max pulled away. "Time's moving on, Laura. You okay to get going?"

He turned his torch on her and she nodded, and then grimaced as the memory of the squeeze spaces returned. "Through those tiny spaces again?"

"I think we'll leave those behind. There's another way. A way I think you'll approve of. Come on, I'll show you."

They walked carefully along the slippery rocks to where the water rushed by and disappeared down into the rock. There were rubber rings stacked to one side.

"Ever heard of black water rafting?" he asked.

Her laughter echoed around them, filling the space with the sound of pure relief.

Fully recovered, Laura did a bit of filming before climbing into her rubber ring. She fixed her GoPro onto her helmet alongside the torch and grinned at Max who was getting into his. Holding tightly on to the sides, with one guide in the front, Max and the other guide behind, they were off, shooting through the fast-moving water, the darkness punctuated by the shifting lights from the top of their helmets.

Despite these lights, Laura was overwhelmed by the darkness, and the power of the rock and the rushing water, the currents of air rushing past her face. She'd never known anything like it—in equal parts terrifying and awe-inspiring. They bumped against rocks, protected by the inflatable rings. At times the ceiling was low and her light revealed scrapes from helmets when the water must have been at a higher level. She thanked God that there had been little rain recently and the water was running low.

She thought she'd never forget that short time, spent rapidly descending through the mountain. The sheer thrill, unnerving darkness, shifting images as the lights on their helmets illuminated different parts of the caves, of each other, of the way ahead, all at once as each of them twisted and raced down the column of swiftly flowing water.

Then, suddenly, before she was ready, a light appeared, rapidly increasing in size and the water shot out of it and dumped them into the river. They all laughed as they drifted toward the shore.

Laura was trembling as she stepped out.

Max helped her. "Are you okay?"

"I've never been so scared, or so thrilled, in all my life."

"Cool. Job done, then."

IT WASN'T UNTIL LATER, at dinner, that Max asked the question which had been bugging him ever since they'd returned from caving. They weren't alone but at least they were out of earshot of anyone else.

"Are you going to tell me what that was all about?"

Laura looked up with a false expression of inquiry, which he'd come to realize she used whenever she wanted to avoid an issue. "What was what all about?"

"Laura McKinney. We may not have known each other long but sometimes I reckon I know you better than most people—Kelly excluded. But you're hiding something, something which you're avoiding thinking about."

"Is that right?" She smiled at the waiter and asked for a top up of water. They exchanged a few words and Laura signed a napkin, ostensibly for the waiter's daughter, but Max doubted it. There seemed to be no age limits to people susceptible to Laura's charm. She turned back to Max with a smile. She lifted her glass of Champagne. "So what are we drinking to tonight?"

He sat back and considered her. She'd be gone in a few short months. He could let it go. He didn't need to go deeper with her. But, as the silence lengthened and her eyes flashed with something like nervousness, he knew he had to.

He raised his glass. "The truth. Can you accept that as a challenge?"

She kept her eyes on his. "Of course. You know me." Her lips twisted into a wry smile. "The truth!" They clinked glasses and she sat back in her chair and crossed her arms in a defensive gesture.

He sat forward, elbows on the table. It unnerved her further. Good. "What made you so scared down there?"

She shrugged lightly. "In the cave? Who doesn't have a few irrational fears?"

"*You* don't."

Her lip trembled slightly and then she did something she never did. She averted her gaze.

He reached forward and took her hands in his. A dozen flash lights lit the restaurant. Startled, he glanced around. He'd forgotten the paparazzi were still around. Laura didn't appear to notice. It was back to front, he thought. She only noticed things when she was alone.

"It was so dark when our lamps went out. I want to feel things, you know? I go out of my way to feel, but when it's dark… it's like there's nothing left. All I feel is empty. All I feel…" She looked up with tears in her eyes. It shocked him more than anything. "Is the opposite of alive."

"Ah," he said. Something slotted into place. Not the last piece, for sure. But something that made the puzzle that was Laura, more understandable.

"It makes sense. Sensory deprivation is used in torture."

"But I'm not being tortured."

"Aren't you?"

"What do you mean?"

"Seems to me like you're torturing yourself."

"Thanks for the analysis. But I'm fine. Nothing I can't handle."

He paused and thought back to what she'd told him about her past. "So… how long is it since you were sick?"

She sighed. "I don't know what made me tell you that. I shouldn't have."

"Yes, you should. I'm not going to tell anyone. I'm simply trying to understand. How long?"

"Around five years."

"And you've been moving around for?"

"five years."

"What is it you're looking for?"

She sat back and opened her arms, exasperated. "Isn't that obvious?"

"Not to me, it's not."

"I want to feel *alive*… I want to feel *everything*."

"And it's working okay? This feeling 'alive' and then moving on. Never stopping to look at yourself. You know, I don't think I've ever seen you look in the mirror."

A flare of panic lit her eyes. She shrugged. "So?"

"It's pretty unusual for a beautiful woman not to ever look in the mirror."

She didn't speak and he suddenly realized he still had hold of her hands.

"Laura. I'm sorry for probing, but I want to get to the bottom of this because I feel there's something you're running from."

"But that's not your problem. I'll be gone soon."

"So there's no point in hiding anything from me. I like you. I *really* like you. Why not open up? You never know, it might help."

"Help you or me?"

"You."

"I don't like seeing my image in the mirror. It makes me panic." She mumbled the words, sending darting looks across the room as she spoke. "I know it's weird. I make a joke of it to Kelly, but it's real."

He was surprised but he didn't show it. "What do you see when you look in the mirror?"

"I see someone who looks like me but who isn't me. I don't know who it is." Her eyes were wide with fear.

"I don't know what that means. But I sure as hell can find out. But I'd bet whatever you like, that it's associated with your illness. You've been running from yourself. You need to stop."

As Laura rose to talk with some of her fans, Max sat back and watched her. He'd gotten closer to understanding her. For all her beauty and bravery, she was wounded at the core. He'd known something was amiss from day one and it had intrigued him. Now he'd uncovered it he'd discovered, to his dismay, that while the intrigue had been solved, his need to do something about it hadn't. He was in deeper than he'd imagined.

9

"A FAMILY WEDDING! WILL LAURA STOP
AVOIDING HER GORGEOUS HUSBAND AND
ACCEPT THE INVITATION?"
@TELLTALEGIRL #ANOTHERWEDDING

*M*ax tapped the gold-embossed invitation against the back of his old sofa. Seems he wasn't the only one with marriage on his mind. His sister Lizzi and good mate, Pete, hadn't wasted any time before becoming engaged and he and Laura were invited to the wedding at Akaroa at the weekend. He'd go—he wouldn't miss it for the world. But Laura? He had no idea. As soon as they'd returned from the caving trip, she'd disappeared—out chasing challenges, trouble and avoiding anything that smacked of emotional issues. And not necessarily in that order.

He knew the trip had affected her deeply and he'd hoped she'd open up about her problems. He knew they had no future, but during the few months they'd be together he'd hoped to get to know her better, and maybe even help her to face whatever was bugging her. But she'd run. And Max had no clue when he'd see her again.

When he'd received the invitation he'd let Kelly know, but Kelly had been evasive about Laura's movements. And he hadn't received a reply from Laura. He'd had enough.

He grabbed his phone and sent a text through to Lizzi. He'd respond to the invitation. Only him, not Laura. Besides, he thought, chances were that Laura and her entourage would derail the wedding. It was Lizzi's day and he wanted only the best for his kid sister. He shot another text through to Kelly before tossing down the phone. Job done.

~

LAURA FLOPPED down into the chair and stretched her aching limbs. Weird, she hadn't felt this tired in years. Must be all this aggro she was receiving from Kelly.

"Satisfied?" asked Kelly, twisting the screen so Laura could see the comments streaming through on her YouTube channel. Laura glanced over and looked away. She didn't like reading the comments which called into question her relationship with Max, not least because she agreed with them. She *was* avoiding him—but not for the reasons her fans were putting forward.

"It's fine. They'll come round."

"You think?" Kelly rose and came over to Laura. "You're not invincible! Your career could stop just like that." She snapped her fingers. "And then what?"

"And then…" She shrugged. "I'll do something different."

Kelly gripped Laura by her shoulders. "You have to listen to me. You can't keep on running. I thought this time, with Max, you might actually accept the challenge of allowing yourself to feel something for someone."

Laura frowned. "The challenge was nothing about feeling, it was about marriage."

Kelly shook her head and let Laura go. "Only *you* could think that they were two different things."

Laura didn't reply because Kelly was wrong. Laura might have thought once that they were different things, but not now. She *did* feel things for Max, things she didn't want to feel, things she was determined to walk away from.

"We've got to put this right, Laura. No more running away. Now, Max has declined an invitation for you to attend Lizzi and Pete's wedding in Akaroa."

Laura looked up, all attention. "Lizzi? Akaroa? Oh!" The strength of the appeal of seeing Max's siblings again, as well his father, and Akaroa, surprised Laura.

"Well you can't. He's right. You'd attract too much attention and that's not what Max wants for his sister."

Laura pursed her lips in regret and rubbed her forehead. "I'd have liked to have gone."

"If you hadn't ignored my emails, you'd have known about the invitation. Anyway, I'm surprised. Why do you want to see Max? You've been avoiding him these past weeks."

Laura shrugged. "I don't know... It's just... Anyhow, I'll be leaving soon, so I guess a weekend in Akaroa would be nice. I won't see him after we return to the States." She narrowed her gaze onto Kelly. "I do *have* some other stuff coming up in the States, don't I?"

Kelly was suddenly busy. "No, nothing planned."

"How come?"

Kelly shrugged and then looked at her directly. "You're avoiding the issue. What are you going to do about Max?"

Laura folded her arms angrily. "What do you suggest?"

"See him when he returns from Akaroa. Spend time with him. As you say, you've only a few more weeks left then it'll all be over. If you want it to be..." She trailed off.

"If I want it to be? What do you mean? Do you really think I should continue this charade?"

Kelly gazed at her directly, quietly. "Only if you cease to make it a charade."

Laura sighed. "I like him. You know I like him."

"Then spend some time with him."

"It's difficult. Things have become more... intense between us."

"That's good."

"No, it's not."

"All I'm saying is, just continue this marriage without an agenda, just enjoy his company, just..."

Kelly was never at a loss for words. She didn't hesitate about anything. Laura searched her best friend's face and something clicked. "You want me to fall in love with him, don't you?"

Kelly pulled away from her and didn't meet her gaze. "Why would I want you to do that?"

"I don't know. You tell me."

"It doesn't matter what I want, or don't want, it's what *you* want."

"What I want is to get out of here as soon as possible."

As soon as she'd said the words, she regretted it. Not only because it wasn't true but also because she sounded like a woman she wouldn't have liked to know—someone hard, someone unfeeling, someone who she didn't recognize.

"Fine," said Kelly, as she slammed some papers onto the desk. "Leave it with me. We'll be on the first plane out of here after your marriage has been annulled."

"Good." But Laura didn't move after Kelly left the room. She continued to look out to the mountains, the blue, blue sky, but she saw none of it. She simply thought of Max. She *would* leave. But there was something she needed—no, *wanted* —to do first.

LAURA THANKED the driver and slammed the car door shut. She wished she'd gone with Kelly's suggestion of hiring a driver instead of hitch-hiking. She felt exhausted as the truck drove off down the dusty road. She turned to the Connelly family home—Belendroit—which peeped out from behind a thicket of trees behind a picket fence which had seen better days. A gate stood permanently open, the tree to which it had been fixed now a part of it.

She might not be able to see anything, but she could hear. Music drifted out to the road, along with a low hum of laughter and talk. She suddenly felt unsure. All the way here, hitchhiking, disguised from her fans by the wig and boho hippy clothes Kelly had picked up for her from a charity shop, she'd felt like she was on another of her challenges. But now she'd arrived and she suddenly felt like an outsider. Would Max welcome her, let alone any of his family?

A frisbee suddenly burst through the trees and onto the drive. Laura smiled and walked into the drive way and picked it up. It felt like a sign, an invitation. Two cocker spaniels came running up, barking at her. She took aim and threw the frisbee into the garden, under the trees. The dogs ran off in hot pursuit. Laura turned around and saw a red-headed young woman approaching her with a big wide smile.

"Hey there!" she greeted. "You don't look like the paparazzi. Are you?"

"No," Laura laughed. "I actually have an invitation to the wedding. Do you want to see it?" She rummaged around in her old ruck-sack.

"No, don't worry about it. You don't look like someone we should be scared of. Come on down. The ceremony's about to begin." They fell into step. "It got delayed as Max had to throw a couple of reporters out. They were pretending to be guests but I could tell they weren't as soon as I saw them."

Laura's heart sank. It was her fault. She only hoped her notoriety hadn't spoiled anything for Lizzi or Pete.

"I love your dress, by the way. I can't wear orange. With my hair I look like I'm on fire."

"That sounds a pretty good look to me."

"And the hat. Very cool."

"Thanks. We found them in an op shop." She plucked at the blood orange cheesecloth material.

"Well, they look good on you." The stranger paused and gave an enchanting smile of pure welcome. Laura relaxed. This woman was impossible not to like. "Which one of us invited you?"

"Max."

"Max?" Amber stopped where the trees thinned out and the house became visible. She frowned. "That's not cool."

"Why not?"

"Because he's married and she couldn't be here today because of the publicity. Max said she didn't want to take attention away from the bride and groom. He said she was pretty sweet that way. And yet he invited you?"

Laura smiled, her mind having stopped on Max's comment about her being sweet. He'd never said anything like that to her and she never thought of herself in those terms. It made her *feel* sweet.

"Yes."

"What did you say your name was?"

Suddenly Max appeared on the veranda, did a double-take and came toward her. Amber saw Max approach at the same time and looked back at Laura. Laura took off her sunglasses and grinned at Amber. She lifted the long dark wig she wore to reveal her blonde hair and pressed her finger to her lips.

Amber laughed and grabbed her arm as they went to meet Max. "Don't worry, I won't say a word."

.   .   .

WHEN MAX HAD FIRST SEEN Amber talking to the dark-haired hippy in the drive, he'd thought it was another Laura groupie who had to be driven off. But then she'd laughed at something Amber said and he'd known. She might be able to disguise herself by her different style, wig, hat and glasses, but not her laugh.

"Laura." He nodded as he approached her.

"Max," replied Laura. "I hope it's okay…me coming, I mean."

He was surprised by how uncertain she appeared. It wasn't like her. Before he could answer, Amber looked from one to the other and slipped her arm through Laura's. It appeared Amber, as she did with most people, had already taken Laura into her heart.

"She's in disguise, Max, so don't spoil it," said Amber. "You never know, there might be a journalist lurking in the trees somewhere just waiting for this moment."

"And I really don't want to start anything," added Laura.

"Then why did you come?" He knew the words sounded harsh but Laura had been avoiding him for weeks and he wanted to know the answer. But she didn't answer, simply met his gaze in an uncomfortable impasse.

"Shut up, Max!" said Amber. "Look! Things are about to start. Go away, and leave Laura with me. You're the best man, you need to be over there with Pete."

There was never any point in arguing with Amber because usually there was little logic to be followed and Amber did her own thing anyway. Not that it ever stopped him. But, for once, as Max left the two of them and walked over to where Pete stood, tugging at his tie, looking the most nervous he'd ever seen him, Max had to admit, Amber had a point. Besides he was here for Lizzi.

As if conjured by his thoughts, Lizzi appeared as the music began. She walked up the short grassy path from the house on the arm of a proud, dapper looking Jim Connelly, with Lizzi's daughter, Aimee, walking ahead, sprinkling rose petals as she went. He'd never seen Lizzi look more beautiful, or more serenely happy and it filled him with a deep sense of contentment. Being the eldest of a large family he'd always felt responsible for his siblings. And when, too late, he'd discovered what Lizzi had suffered at the hands of her first husband, he'd also felt guilt—guilt that he hadn't known and hadn't sorted out her problems. But she'd dealt with all that on her own and, now, one glance at Pete told him that he didn't have to worry about her anymore. She had a happy future ahead of her.

But as soon as the marriage celebrant began speaking, he was forced to remember another wedding ceremony. His own. He continued to focus on Lizzi and Pete as they spoke their vows to each other—vows which he knew no one had created for them, because they came straight from the heart. The contrast to the debacle of his own wedding, to how he now felt about Laura, got to him and he could no longer avoid looking at her. He glanced to one side and caught her gaze.

Apart from him and Laura, there wasn't a dry eye in the house. And that wasn't because they weren't moved, he knew that much. He could see it in Laura's devastated gaze, and he felt it deep in his heart. This was marriage; this was the real thing and what they'd done was a travesty of everything his family—and his mother—held dear. How had they both got it so wrong?

IT WASN'T until much later, after the reception which was held in the gardens, after all the speeches had been made, after more laughter and some tears, that Max sought out Laura. They'd been seated at opposite ends of the table so as not to arouse any speculation. He'd been aware of her, how could he not be? Even if she was, to her credit, keeping in the background.

But it hadn't only been that which had stopped him from talking to her. She'd been avoiding him for weeks and now she was here, apparently expecting to be welcomed with open arms. But he wasn't in the mood for being relegated to being one of her hangers-on—there when she wanted him to be, but absent when it suited. Life wasn't like that; *he* wasn't like that. Not with her, anyway.

He looked around. She wasn't with Amber and Aimee who were playing with the dogs on the veranda, and she wasn't with the others on the beach. He went inside the house which was quiet and which he noticed for the first time, had a neglected feel. He shrugged it off. No doubt a contrast to the busyness and fun outside.

He went inside the sunny kitchen-diner, and looked out the window.

Most people had moved off down to the beach from where he could hear shouts of laughter and splashing. He glanced out the window just in time to see Pete drop his bride, Lizzi, into the water from the old jetty. He smiled to himself. Pete had a lot to learn. Max knew that Lizzi would get her own back and some—but Pete would never know when it was going to happen. Max grinned.

"You have one big happy family," said Laura, as she came and stood beside him, holding a bottle of sparkling wine and two champagne flutes.

He turned to look at her fully for the first time. She'd taken off her hat and her blonde hair was messy and tousled, falling around her tanned shoulders. She looked out the window at his family and friends doing what they've always done for half the year—fooling around in the bay.

"Mostly," he said, forcing himself to look away from her pretty face, freckled nose, fresh complexion, no make-up as usual.

"A glass of bubbly?" she offered, setting them onto a nearby table and pouring a glass.

"Sure, thanks," he said, accepting the glass.

She poured another for herself and held it up to him with her head cocked to one side, but her face serious.

"Here's to marriage," he said, clinking his glass against Laura's.

"To marriage." She sipped the wine. "Two weddings within a few months of each other. That's quite something."

"Yes. But they're not in the same league though, are they?"

"True. Lizzi and Pete look totally in love."

"And we weren't."

Laura looked away quickly.

"They're in it for the long haul, whatever happens."

"Yeah." Max glanced at them. "Pete will look after her."

"I think they'll look after each other." Laura raised an eyebrow. "Looking after someone isn't the male prerogative, you know."

"Yeah, I know. But I'm old-fashioned about some things. Sometimes women need to be protected, to be cared for, and cherished."

"And men? Don't they need the same thing?"

"Not so much. We're a tough lot."

She snaked her finger up his arm. "Is that so? You mean you don't feel anything when I do this?" She looped her finger under his shirt and tickled his forearm.

He shook his head at her flirtation but didn't fool himself it meant anything. "Sure do. Feels like a spider's crept up my shirt."

She cocked her head to one side. "A spider, eh? Well, how about this?" She tightened her fingers around his arm and pulled him toward her. She licked her lips and stood on tiptoe and kissed the corner of his mouth. He sucked in a harsh breath and turned his head to try to capture her mouth with his but she pulled away, laughing. "Hm, I wonder what else you feel?"

"Come to my room tonight and I'll show you."

Her face suddenly lost its humor. "I... I'm not sure if I'll be able to stay."

He frowned. "How did you get here, by the way? I don't see any cars I don't recognize."

"I hitch-hiked."

"You what?"

She smiled. "Hitch-hiked. You know, you stick up your thumb in the air when a car comes past. And hope they'll stop."

"You hitch-hiked?" he said, exploding all over again as his mind ran over the risks she'd run.

She laughed but this time it didn't amuse him.

"You're crazy!"

"And you're only just finding that out?"

"But anything could have happened to you!"

"And anything did. Two lovely couples gave me lifts. One from Queenstown to Christchurch and then another to here."

He shook his head, unable to express how much he hated the thought of her hitch-hiking.

"It was the only way, Max! I got my disguise together. Kelly gave me a lift to the main road and then I was off."

He watched her as she looked around. Even with the flowing clothes that hid her beautiful body she looked amazing. He suddenly realized that this was because she *was* completely amazing to him.

"Stay the night, Laura."

"I couldn't impose. Besides there's probably no room."

"There's room in my bed."

She bit her lip and shook her head.

"No, of course, not," he said quickly. "You know, I don't want to take anything you don't want to give."

"You mean sex."

He sighed. "No, I don't mean just sex. People are chasing you all the time, wanting something from you, a smile, a photo, to talk to you. But that's not me. You're welcome to stay the night, lay beside me on my bed and I will hold you, simply hold you, just as I did the night we married. Just stay, Laura, give this thing we have going between us a chance, see where it takes us."

She bit her lip and then shook her head. "No, I can't."

"Right. That smacks of intimacy and you don't do that, do you, Laura? Physical or emotional. You came close to it in the caves and I didn't see you for weeks afterward. Tell me, why the hell did you come here, anyway?"

"I wanted to be here, to see everyone."

"To flirt with me a bit, maybe to kiss… but no more than that, eh, Laura? Because that's as far as you go. At the smallest sign of anything more, you're off."

Laura's smile vanished. "That's not true!"

"I think it is. You've made it clear you don't want to go anywhere near intimacy—emotional or otherwise. You're scared. I get that, but—"

"I am *not* scared! I'm not scared of anything! How can you believe that after all the challenges I've accepted, all the challenges I've succeeded at? No, I simply don't want a relationship. I've spent my whole adult life on my own, looking after myself. It's enough for me. It *has* to be enough."

"Okay, have it your own way. So, in a few months we'll get the marriage annulled as arranged."

She glanced away and didn't answer.

"That *is* what you want, isn't it, Laura?"

She shrugged. "That's what we agreed."

They stared at each other again and it was Max who turned away first. He was desperately disappointed and he didn't want Laura to see it. He'd thought maybe she'd come to the wedding with the intention of turning their marriage into something more meaningful. But he was wrong. She'd felt trapped by not being able to come here, trapped by her own fame and had created her own challenge, her own little drama, including a disguise and hitchhiking, to get here. No doubt there would be much mileage and hilarity to be made of it on her return.

She began to walk away but stopped and turned.

"I can't do intimacy, Max, you should know that much about me."

He shrugged, and stuck his hands in his pockets. "That's fine. Walk away then. But I need something first."

"What?"

"The ring. It might not mean anything to you, but it sure means something to me."

"Of course." She tried to pull the ring off but it wouldn't shift. "It won't come." She pulled again. "My stupid fingers. They're still swollen for some reason."

He frowned. "Let me see." He took her hand in his and studied it. "It *is* swollen. Why, what's up?"

"I don't know, just hot I guess."

"Leave it then. I guess we need to continue to fool your precious public, even if we're no longer fooling ourselves."

"Don't, Max. Please."

He could see Laura was close to tears. Reluctantly he let her hand slip through hers. His fingers extending at the last moment as if reluctant to lose contact.

She stepped away, bringing her arm abruptly by her side. "I'm sorry, Max. But I feel strange. I need to get out of here."

"You mean you feel you need to get away from me."

"No, I can't seem to see clearly. I feel dizzy."

She looked around as if her vision had truly been affected. "You don't need to do this charade for me. I get it. Go. Why don't you just go?"

"Sure. I'll..." She turned away and stumbled down the steps and ran across the lawn, pushing her way past people, including Rachel who frowned and came up to Max.

"What's wrong with Laura? She looked pretty distressed."

"Sure she is. I told her that I didn't want her to leave. I told her that I wanted to see if this thing we had could go anywhere. I asked her to stay."

"My God, Max! I think it's *you* who are under the weather." Rachel gaped at him, then turned to see Laura disappearing along the path up to the road. Then back to him. "And she said no?"

"I'm not sure she even got that far. It seemed the thought of being with me disturbed her so much that she felt ill and she couldn't get away fast enough." Max turned his back on where Laura had disappeared. He didn't need to see her absence to feel the pain.

"But that's not like her to face up to it."

"She faces up to everything except what's inside her."

"But she likes you. Anyone can see that. More than likes. Lizzi and I were thinking you guys could make a go of this, despite how it started."

"And so did I, Rachel, so did I."

"What did she say exactly?"

He shrugged. "What does it matter?"

"Tell me."

"That she couldn't see properly. That she felt peculiar."

Rachel frowned. "And you let her go?"

"She'd made it pretty plain that that's exactly what she wanted to do."

"Are you sure she wasn't *really* feeling ill? I know you guys always like to think *everything*, every reaction is caused by something you've said or done. But, you know sometimes, it *is* what it *is*."

"What the hell are you talking about?"

"She might be sick. Go, check up on her. Anyhow, she's just walked up to the road. How do you think she's going to get anywhere at this time of the evening? There's no passing traffic, there's no public transport. She's used to having everything laid on. Go. Now. Make sure she's okay."

"Are you kidding me? If I go after her now I'll be had up for harassment!"

"Go. Or I will." She glared at him.

But it wasn't what Rachel had said which made him move. He'd been ignoring it but somewhere he *was* unsettled; somewhere there was a low sound of a warning bell ringing.

He walked out the front door, glanced around the veranda and then ran down the front steps onto the front lawn which led to the woods and driveway onto the road. He walked up the potholed drive, wondering for the nth time why his father didn't do usual fatherly things like keep the house and estate in order.

The drive was empty. He arrived at the road which was also empty. He turned around, and scratched his head. She'd vanished into thin air.

Then he heard a dog bark, followed by another. Stanley, Boo—what were they barking at? He retraced his steps. The barking was coming from the middle of the woods—equally unkempt, equally wild. He batted away some dangling creepers and stepped through the undergrowth. The barking grew louder. It was coming from the very heart of the wood. They must have cornered a rabbit or something. He'd sort them out before they disturbed the wedding party, then he'd return to the party. Laura must have returned to it around the other way.

"Stan!" Max shouted. "Here, boy!"

But no Stan emerged.

Max pressed on through the tangle of briars and overgrown bushes toward where the barking was coming from. "Stan!" He stepped forward to where Stanley stood barking above a lump on the ground. Boo wasn't barking, she was prodding or licking something. What the heck?

He stepped forward and his blood froze. There on the ground was Laura, lying on her side, her face deathly pale, her eyelids fluttering.

"Laura?"

She groaned and closed her eyes. She was barely conscious. He knelt beside her and felt for her pulse—it was weak. Both dogs stood back, allowing the recognized pack leader to sort out the problem. He lifted her up and accompanied by the two dogs, carried her back to the house. Rachel had appeared, obviously wondering about Laura, and immediately ran over to them.

"She's collapsed. Her pulse is weak. Get Gabe. Then dial emergency services and tell them we'll get her to Christchurch hospital by helicopter. It'll be quicker than them sending an ambulance."

By the time he'd walked her into the house and lain her down on the chaise longue in the drawing room, Gabe had appeared and took over. Max stood back and let Gabe do the necessary checks, stunned and appalled by what had happened.

"Has she taken any drugs?" asked Gabe, as he checked her pulse.

"No way. She doesn't take drugs. She hardly drinks alcohol."

Gabe closed his eyes as he pressed his fingers to her pulse. "Something's affected her heart. Sounds like she has a murmur. Could be related to her rheumatic fever." He looked up at Max "Do you know if she contracted an infection recently?"

Max frowned, trying to think. "She said she had a tooth abscess in Australia. But it healed, I think."

Gabe grimaced. "Could be infective endocarditis."

"What's that?"

"Serious, is what that is. She needs to get to a hospital fast."

Rachel appeared.

"Have you contacted emergency services?" asked Gabe.

"Yes, but they agree with Max. It'll be quicker for us to fly her there."

"Then let's get on with it. Max can fly while I take care of Laura. You'd best come too. Grab some essentials, Rach, and let's get going."

Max picked Laura back up again as Rachel gathered things under Max's direction. Jim Connelly entered the room, closely followed by Lizzi and Pete. "What the hell's happened to Laura?"

"She's collapsed. That's all we know. Something to do with her heart. We're taking her to Christchurch now."

"Poor kid," said Jim. "But she's in good hands with you."

Max didn't have time to express his surprise at his father's words. He continued straight out the door.

"Do you want a hand?" called Pete, from behind.

"Just look after things here, thanks mate."

By the time he'd crossed the road to the paddock which he used as a helicopter pad, both Rachel and Gabe had joined him from different directions, both carrying what they needed for the journey.

Reluctantly Max relinquished Laura into Gabe's care

while he concentrated on getting them to Christchurch as soon as they could.

The flight was intense as the three siblings conversed in short, to the point, comments, all focusing on what they needed to do to keep Laura alive, to get her help as soon as they could. It was a short flight but it felt as if it were going on forever to Max.

He remained focused on flying the helicopter. They all depended on him and he suppressed everything—every fear, every regret, every feeling he had for the woman who lay lifeless in the back seat—so he could focus on what had to be done to get her help.

Max spoke over the radio. He turned it off, and spoke to Gabe and Rachel, through their headphones. "We'll be landing in five minutes. They have emergency services waiting for us. They want to know if there's anything further we can tell them. Gabe?"

Gabe reeled off her vital signs and then paused.

"Right," said Max. "Anything else?"

"Tell them that I think she has heart failure. Class 4. Severe."

"LAURA'S HEART HAS BROKEN AND SO HAS
ALL OF OURS…GET WELL…" @TELLTALEGIRL
#HEARTSICK

*M*ax heard the words "heart failure", but refused to understand them. They sat on the edge of his consciousness as he continued to focus on flying the helicopter. They were words without meaning, words that needed to be kept at arm's length because he dared not understand them, dared not let the meaning penetrate his mind, or his heart. Because he didn't know what would happen if he did.

Instead, he flexed his hands over the controls as he circled once around Hagley Park, opposite the hospital, and came into land. With studied detachment he watched the hospital orderlies run toward the helicopter as Rachel slammed open the door. The doctor peered in, exchanged a few words with Gabe and then gave the word for the orderlies to move Laura, who was still semi-conscious, onto a stretcher. Everything happened quickly after that. Gabe followed Rachel and the medics across the grass towards the hospital. Max craned his neck, trying to catch sight of Laura but she was surrounded by medics. An official signaled to Max. His prompt to take off again, to leave the space clear for other incoming emergencies. It was time to go, time to leave Laura with the people who could help her.

He eased the throttle on the helicopter and rose into the air. He glanced once at the bustling crowd which now surrounded Laura as it moved toward the open doors of the hospital. He couldn't see her. *He couldn't see her*, he thought, suddenly panicked. But, as he twisted the helicopter around in the direction of the airport, he thought he *would* see her, and when he did he wouldn't leave her side.

IT WAS an hour before Max could return to the hospital. For most of the taxi drive from the airport he'd stared out at the flat suburban landscape, trying to hold on to the thought that Laura was in the best of hands, and that this was a nightmare from which he'd soon awake. The one phone call he'd had with Gabe hadn't brought good news. Laura was undergoing tests and there'd been no change in her condition.

Self-recrimination, guilt, anger with himself, even anger with Laura, filled him. But not as much as grief. And that grief put everything into perspective. That grief spelled things out so clearly that he thought he must have been blind before. He had feelings for her which went deeper than any he'd experienced before and, if she survived this, he'd make sure he'd do everything in his power to make her happy.

It was nearly eight in the evening by the time he arrived at the hospital. Gabe was pacing the floor while Rachel stared blankly at a magazine. They both looked at him with something like relief in their eyes. Of course, Max thought, people always looked to him to save the situation. How come he could fool everyone so effectively, make them believe he was invincible, when he couldn't even look after the woman who'd quickly come to mean everything to him?

"Any news?" he asked.

"No," they both said, sitting down again.

"Why don't you guys go home? Go back to Belendroit. Dad will be worrying."

"No way. We'll stay with you. Won't we, Gabe?"

"Of course." Gabe gripped Max's shoulder. "We're here for you, bro."

Max hardly felt Gabe's grip. He looked at him bleakly and wondered if he'd feel anything again because, beside Laura's collapse, nothing was important, nothing could touch him.

MAX GLANCED AGAIN at the clock which had moved on precisely five minutes since he'd last looked. It was three in the morning and Max was still numb, still sitting on the same hard-backed chair he'd sat on when he'd first entered the hospital.

He hadn't paced the floor, hadn't bitten his nails, talked, fiddled with his phone—anything. All his energy had turned inward. He simply sat, alternately staring at his hands and the clock, focusing on Laura, visualizing every life-affirming aspect of her—from her laugh which caught people up in her energy, to the unself-conscious way she presented her natural sexiness, to her fearlessness. He'd once read somewhere that if you gave something or someone attention then you strengthened the subject of your thoughts. It was all he could do for Laura now.

Rachel was curled up asleep on a couple of chairs and the only sign Gabe was asleep was his closed eyes and regular breathing. Otherwise, Gabe sat the same way—legs outstretched, hands loosely clenched in front of him. Max idly wondered if Gabe ever let loose his restraint. He was always so measured, so reasonable in everything. Max wished he had an ounce of that containment, or reason. If he had, Laura might not be lying in intensive care right now.

Max moved onto the third cup of powdered coffee from the machine down the hall and Gabe awoke and looked immediately at him.

"Any news?"

Max shook his head.

Gabe stretched and walked over and drank some of Max's coffee and gave it back to him with a grimace. "That is really bad coffee. In fact it shouldn't be dignified with the name 'coffee.'"

Max shrugged. "I haven't thought about the taste." Strange how all his senses seemed to have deserted him except one—his ability to remember everything about Laura. And those memories stripped his heart bare. Nothing—no taste, no sight, no sound, came close to the enormity of what her collapse had awakened in his heart. He knew with absolute clarity that nothing would be the same again.

"I should have guessed from her hands."

Max looked at his brother. "What?"

"Her hands. They'd swollen. Remember? She told me that they'd swollen suddenly and she couldn't get Mum's ring off her finger."

"Oh my God! Of course."

"Yeah," said Gabe bleakly. "Fluid retention is a sign that the heart isn't working. I didn't pick it up."

"Why would you? You weren't looking for it. And she was so fit the other symptoms were probably hidden."

Suddenly the doors opened. Gabe looked up and Max leaped to his feet, spilling the coffee.

"How is she?"

"She's awake now. She's out of danger." The doctor looked at Gabe. "You were correct in your diagnosis, doctor. If you hadn't been so prompt we might not have been able to save her in time."

"Heart failure?" asked Max, still unable to believe his vital

Laura could be subject to such a devastating thing.

"Yes. The good news is that the treatment is straightfor-ward. Antibiotics, and she's responding well."

"Thank God." Then Max swallowed, realizing there must be some bad news to follow. "But?"

"But…" The doctor inhaled, as if playing for time. "This was a serious episode and we can't predict what damage her heart has sustained, or its impact on her future. The MRI and scans show that the scarring on the valves of her heart has worsened with this infection. She'll need surgery if she's not to relapse."

"Surgery?" said Max, grasping at something solid he could deal with that would solve things. "We'll organize surgery. And that will fix it?"

"There's never any guarantees. But it's certainly the best option. It has a high success rate."

"Good." Max paced, stopped and shook the doctor's hand. "Thank you."

He watched the doctor leave and turned to the others who were staring at him. "Did you hear that?" His voice cracked and Max suddenly felt overwhelmed. Tense all night, it was like the doctor had flicked a switch, unraveling the cord that had kept him together. He sat down as if pushed and doubled over, putting his head in his hands, willing the tears that sprung into his eyes to disappear. What the hell? He never cried. But it was like trying to shore up a tsunami and before he knew it his shoulders were shuddering and he was sobbing like a child.

"Christ!" said Gabe. "Rach?" he called, the fear evident in his voice.

"Max!"

Max felt Rachel's arms come around him and he slumped against her, allowing her to comfort him in a way she'd never done before, in a way he'd never needed her to do before.

"It's okay, Max. *She'll* be okay. You heard what the doctor said," said Rachel soothingly.

Max's lungs tried to suck in the air like there wasn't enough of it in the room. What the hell was happening to him? He panicked and pushed Rachel away and jumped up, wiping his face on the back of his sleeve. He paced the room, breathing deeply, trying to calm down. By the time he was steady enough to face Rachel and Gabe, they were both staring at him—Rachel with an expression of tenderness, as if she'd just witnessed the birth of a baby, and Gabe with amused bewilderment.

"Man, you've got it bad!" said Gabe.

Max turned sharply to him. "I don't know what the hell you're talking about." He felt around in his pocket for a handkerchief but he didn't have one. Rachel thrust some tissues into his hand. He blew his nose. "Gabe, do you know about this operation the doctor talked about?"

"A little. There'll be a waiting list."

"No there won't. I'll pay to get it done as soon as possible."

"And there will be recuperation time."

"We'll stay at Belendroit. She likes it there. It'll be peaceful and away from all the drama, and close to the hospital."

"Max," said Rachel softly. "I think you're forgetting something."

Was he? "What?"

"Laura. It's up to her. It's *her* life. She might not want to stay at Belendroit. She might want to go back to the US to have the operation. She might want to go back to recuperate."

He looked away from his brother and sister, remembering Laura's last words to him before she ran off. She'd wanted an annulment. But she'd been sick, hadn't she? Surely that would have altered her perception? But he couldn't ignore the sinking feeling inside which told the real truth.

Laura had never veered away from their intention to get the wedding annulled. *He* might have done, but she never had.

"Maybe. But she's sick. She needs help and, for now, I'm going to give it. And, until she tells me to leave her alone, I'm going to be there for her."

Max noticed Rachel and Gabe exchange looks. He wasn't surprised. He'd never felt like this before—so certain, and yet so helpless. He had no alternative but to look after her, whether or not he was welcome, or would be rebuffed. He had no alternative but to make himself vulnerable, because he loved her. Heart and soul. And he'd do anything for her. Even let her go.

THE DOCTOR EMERGED from the swing doors. "She's awake."

Max didn't need any further invitation. He walked through the doors held open by a nurse and found himself looking down at a woman who was a shadow of Laura. Her eyes were closed, her face deathly pale, dark rings under her eyes. His heart missed a beat but that was the last time, he'd make sure of that. He no longer felt tears, just a roaring strength to make sure Laura got well again.

He sat down beside her quietly. He glanced for reassurance at the doctor, who nodded. "She's simply tired."

At the sound of the doctor's voice, Laura's eyes fluttered open, revealing the woman he knew and loved. She gave a hint of a smile. "Max…" Her lips softly came together and opened to express the word that he hardly heard.

He took hold of her hand in both of his. "Laura." He swallowed and bought time by focusing on her hand in his, smoothing over the fingers, the wee callouses created by her extreme sports, and his mother's wedding ring, still firmly stuck on her finger. He took a deep breath and looked into her eyes which were now fluttering open. "How do you feel?"

She gave a weak smile on lips as pale as her skin. "Fine." Her eyelids closed briefly and her pale lips quirked lightly into a smile. "Just another..." She shifted and grimaced.

He leaned toward her. "What? What is it?"

She settled again. "Challenge. Just another challenge."

He grinned, and for a minute thought those traitorous tears would return but he swallowed them back. "Exactly. And you always win your challenges."

She nodded, her eyes never leaving his. "About what I said before..."

He knew what she was about to say but shook his head. "Don't talk, or think about anything else. Just get well." He wished his voice hadn't cracked on the last word.

The doctor moved forward. "We'd better leave Laura to sleep now. She's been through a lot and needs rest."

Max nodded but didn't move, kept stroking her hand. Irrationally, he wanted to stay, holding her, wanting to give her his strength so she could recover. The doctor coughed and raised his eyebrows at Max, indicating he should leave.

Max bent his head to Laura, who he could see was slipping into sleep. "I'll go, Laura. But I'll be back. You need to know that you're not on your own anymore. I'm here for you for as long as you want me to be. Together we'll make you strong again. Okay?"

Her eyes opened and she gave him a glimmer of a smile. "Promise?" she said between barely open lips.

"Promise," he said softly. He bent down and kissed her cheek. By the time he stood up she was asleep. He turned to the waiting doctor. He'd get this sorted and he'd keep his promise. "Doctor? I'd like a few words."

AFTER HE'D TALKED with the doctor and begun the process of arranging the operation which would make Laura well again, he went back into the waiting room. He was surprised to see his father there.

Jim Connelly held up a suitcase. "I've brought you some things."

Max looked blankly at the suitcase.

"I'm afraid Amber packed it so God knows what's inside."

Max nodded distractedly.

"Probably healing crystals rather than anything useful like a toothbrush," said his father with a rueful grimace.

Max nodded again, blinking back the stupid tears which now seemed to be permanently about to flow.

"Max! How is she?"

Max cleared his throat. "She's okay, Dad. She'll be okay. She needs an operation and time to recuperate but it's so much better than—" He couldn't finish the sentence. God knows what would happen to his voice or the damn tears if he did.

His father stepped forward and gave Max a hug. "So much better than it could have been," Jim finished off for him. He stepped away quickly as if he thought Max would push him away. Max might have done once, but he wouldn't have done now.

His father poured himself a coffee and took a sip before speaking again. "You know, she's a fighter, she'll pull through."

"So was Mum, and she didn't."

There was silence and Max regretted his impulse to speak of his mother's death with all its implications of blame on his father.

"No, she didn't. And, as hard as it is for you to understand, that was *not* my fault."

"Did I say it was?"

"No, but that's what you believe."

Max waved his hand. "Now isn't the time to fight."

"I've never wanted to fight with you, believe it or not."

Max didn't believe it and, from his father's face, could see that he'd conveyed his response without speech.

"I spoke to Laura yesterday," Jim continued.

"Yeah, I saw you. On the veranda."

"She's good company—easy to talk to."

Max drew in a deep breath and looked up the ceiling, thinking about Laura's ease in company—from the very young to the old. "Yeah, she is."

"We talked about you, you know."

His father's sharp eyes didn't leave him. "Oh." He looked away. He felt no interest at his father's words. All he could think of was how Laura looked when he'd seen her talking with his father. Her dippy, hippy clothes seemed to fit with Belendroit's eccentricities. But yesterday at Belendroit was a different time—a time when Laura was well.

"Don't you want to know what we talked about?"

"You've told me already. Me."

His father sighed. "One thing's certain—she's a lot easier to talk to than you!"

"Go on then, what did you talk about? Looks like you're going to tell me whether I want to hear or not."

"Damn right! She told me that you're still hurting over your mother's death. She told me that you're too stubborn to make amends, but that you need me, that you love me, despite what you think I've done."

"She told you all that?"

"Yes, she did. You don't give her enough credit for under-standing you. God knows how she managed it. Seems to me you've talked more to that young woman than anyone else in your life—including me, or your brothers or sisters."

"That's because I love her," Max said bleakly.

There was a long silence. "She didn't say anything about love."

"That's because I haven't told her yet and because she doesn't love me. She still wants to get our marriage annulled."

"Are you sure about that? She didn't strike me as if she was talking about a man she was going to walk away from any time soon."

"Well, she was. She was leaving, going back to Queenstown to carry out our last challenge together—the annulment—when she collapsed."

Jim Connelly reached out and gripped his son's shoulder. "Rachel told me the doctors say she'll be okay and you have to believe that."

Max nodded. "I do. I can't imagine this world without her."

Jim smiled sadly and grunted. "It's good to see you in love." He turned to leave.

"Dad?"

Jim turned back to face Max.

"Laura got it wrong. It's not you I blame for Mum's death. It's me. And it was Laura who made me see that."

Before Jim could say anything Max pushed open the door and went to look at Laura through the window. He wasn't allowed in the same room—she needed to sleep—but he had to see her. He had to be near in case she awoke. He needed to prove to her that it wouldn't be like before. She wouldn't be alone this time.

FOR A MOMENT LAURA didn't know where she was. She licked her lips which were dry and cracked. She tried to swallow. Then she felt her body, not with her hands, but with her mind, checking her strength in every part of her.

She felt her chest rise and fall like bellows, sucking the

dry air of the hospital room into her lungs, feeding the blood that the slow rhythm of her traitorous heart pushed through her chest, to her stomach and limbs. There was no longer any pain. She took a long slow breath. *No pain*, she repeated to herself. Then she did what she was truly scared of doing. She flexed her muscles. Not all at once but starting with her legs, from relaxed she stretched out first one leg and then the other. She felt the tug of tubes attached to her hand. Ah, she thought. That's why there's no pain.

She hadn't yet opened her eyes through which bright light penetrated. She knew she could see because she'd seen Max before and had listened to the doctors. What she was scared of was looking upon the world as an invalid once more, because she didn't know how she could cope again. But now she felt her muscles respond to her commands, it was time. She took a deep breath and opened her eyes.

It wasn't what she expected. The brightness which had awoken her was all around. She didn't move her head right away, just squinted as her eyes became accustomed to the light. Then she rolled her head to one side. She was in a bed beside a window overlooking the park. She was drowning in sunlight. The tops of trees were beginning to turn orange as autumn approached. Thank God she could see. When she'd collapsed she hadn't been able to see anything.

It was as if the collapse had heightened her senses. She was aware of everything—every sound, every pulse and movement in her body. She felt as if she were floating on top of the world. She laughed and a tear trickled from her eyes. She closed them. So much sensory overload was hard to adjust to after her body's near total shutdown.

She drifted off to sleep almost straight away, except this time she was dreaming and felt wonderful. She awoke a little later and immediately turned her head to the window. The sun was setting and it filled the room with a rich glow. But it wasn't only the sun that was different. The room *felt* different and she knew she wasn't alone. Lying flat on her back with no pillow, she had only two options. She rolled her head to the other side but only saw the opposite window. She cleared her throat in order to speak but she immediately heard a chair scrape, her hands taken into two warm large hands and held there as Max's face appeared. His eyes were bleary through lack of sleep, yet they still managed to contain an intensity which was completely focused on her. She felt a familiar rush of attraction in response.

She smiled. "You look terrible." She hardly recognized her raspy voice.

His face twisted into a smile of relief or pain, she couldn't tell which. "You look beautiful."

It was her turn to try to laugh but it didn't happen because her throat felt like sandpaper. Max picked up a glass of water. "Let me help you sit up." He took her tenderly in his arms and placed some pillows behind her. She felt a little dizzy for a few seconds and then, relieved that everything was still functioning, she held her hands over his as he tipped the glass of water toward her mouth. She drank the water which had never tasted so delicious. She lay back on the pillows which Max placed under her and saw, for the first time, that in front of her were more windows, and yet more tops of trees above which sunset colors flooded the sky. The wall against which the bed was placed also had two long windows either side of the bed and one doorway.

"I'm an eagle, in a nest."

His mouth twisted again, as if he were trying to control some stray, unwanted emotion. He rubbed her hands in his, as if he were coaxing something tender into life. "I couldn't have my girl trapped, now, could I?"

"Your girl?" She savored the feel of the words on her lips before swallowing. "Am I still?"

"Sure are."

She smiled and closed her eyes, feeling suddenly tired again. Of course Max had too much integrity, was too much a man, to walk away from a problem.

"Laura? How are you feeling?"

She nodded, took a deep breath and opened her eyes, hoping the tears that pooled there wouldn't overflow. She didn't know if she had the strength to wipe them away. Luckily she didn't have to. Max swept them away with a soft cloth. She didn't want to ask but she had to face the truth.

"I've felt better." She swallowed. "Tell me, Max, am I going to recover?"

He gripped her hands more tightly. "Yes," he said with an urgency designed to convince. "Yes! The operation is scheduled for a week's time, providing you're clear of the infection by then."

"The one the doctor told me about?"

"Yes. You've recovered well from the collapse but they need to operate to fix things for good."

She nodded but couldn't prevent the sob sneaking up in her throat. She felt his lips on hers as she closed her eyes. "It'll be fine, Laura. I'll be with you. And your parents will be here when you wake up from the operation. All the people who love you will be here."

"Max?"

"Yes."

"I never did get to fly with you, did I? Remember, fire, earth and wind… you promised me I'd fly in the wind."

"You will. I promise you that, my love."

The doctor came in and gave her a sedative.

Love… Did Max say "love"? It was the last word on her mind as she drifted into a dreamless sleep.

11

"LAURA IS ON THE MEND BUT WHAT
ABOUT HER MARRIAGE? WILL IT LAST?
HOPE SO…" @TELLTALEGIRL
#TOGETHERFOREVER?

*B*y the time Max returned permanently to the Lodge, Queenstown was busy with the beginning of the winter season. The autumn landscape of burned ochre, russet, and gold was now clothed in the white sheen of early snow. It promised to be a good ski season, Max thought, as he looked out across the hills above which icy crags jutted into an electric blue sky. But the thought didn't lift the pall of sadness which lay over him.

He glanced up at the floor to ceiling windows of the loft which rose out of the top of the Lodge, above the now bare branches of the cherry trees. He'd had it built especially for Laura who now lay there, recuperating. She'd exceeded the doctor's expectations and was recovering well. When he remembered the day she'd collapsed—months ago now—he wondered how on earth they'd both managed to make it through. But he knew. Without the love and support of their families, they'd have survived, but not so well.

Laura's parents had come as soon as they heard. They'd been beside her when she'd awoken from the operation, and had continued to be with her afterwards at Belendroit where she'd been transferred to recuperate as soon as she'd been able. It seemed she'd underestimated their love for her. But it was often that way, thought Max, thinking of his own father, and how he'd been there for Max every hour of every day for the past few months. As had all his siblings.

Family... He'd thought he'd been alone; he'd thought wrong.

Max knew neither family's problems would be solved overnight, but it was a beginning. There had been fault on both sides and it had taken Laura's collapse for her family to realize just what they had and how they needed to work at making their relationship whole again. And that meant Laura returning to the US. But not just yet. They had a week left before she flew out.

She was confused, that much he could see. And he wasn't going to make it harder for her. She needed to do this. *That* much, he knew. And then? The rest was up to her.

It had been Laura who'd insisted on spending these last days at Queenstown. And, for the first time since her parents had arrived, he was alone with her. Her parents had gone to Wellington on business and wouldn't be returning until the day before she left. That mean seven nights. Seven nights and six days in which to help her, and to enjoy her, and he meant to make the most of them.

"I'M COMING with you to the States and that's that," said Kelly, crossing her arms and sitting back in her chair. It was all Laura could do not to smile. She knew from the jut of Kelly's jaw that there was nothing Laura could do to change her mind.

Laura pushed herself upright. "It's just..."

Kelly sat forward, staring directly at Laura. "Just what?"

"Just that… you didn't sign up to be with an invalid."

"I don't remember signing up for anything."

"You know what I mean."

"You're talking nonsense. And it's not like you to talk nonsense. Open your laptop."

"What's the point?"

"It's better than sitting here, whining."

"I do *not* whine! I've never whined."

"Well you *are* now. You're feeling sorry for yourself."

"I am not." She frowned, suddenly uncertain. "Am I?"

A smile broke through Kelly's stern expression. "Yes, you are. And you're being uncertain, which isn't like you either. There's only one thing for it."

"To stay in bed?"

"Don't be ridiculous!"

Laura grunted and folded her arms across her chest and looked determinedly out the window, away from Kelly. She was beginning to annoy her now.

Kelly opened her laptop and brought it to the table. "See, here, *this* is what I'm talking about. Your adoring public are waiting to hear from you."

She couldn't resist looking at the screen, despite herself. And what she saw there made her sit bolt upright in bed. "How many comments?"

"Thousands. All wanting to know if you're going to accept your next challenge."

"What challenge?" She started scrolling through the comments, back to the top. "You mean someone's challenged me while I've been lying here sick?"

"Looks like it."

"What kind of person would do a thing like that?"

Kelly shrugged. "Maybe someone who wants to win the challenge?"

"But that *so* isn't fair." She read through the challenge. "How could anyone—" She stopped suddenly as she looked at the person who'd posted it. "Max!" She frowned. "Really? Max?"

"Yep."

She read through the challenge more carefully, aware of the sudden, familiar thrill coursing through her body, just as it always had when she'd read through prospective challenges.

"Wind. The last of the three challenges. Wind. But he's not saying what it is. This is some kind of notice of a challenge. I'm not going to find out what it is until a few hours before it happens. What should I do?"

"Prepare, and then accept it when it comes. Simple."

"No, it's not simple. I'm sick."

"You're not sick anymore. You're on the mend."

"Maybe, but not on the mend enough to deal with a challenge like this. Wind? What can he mean?"

"Only one way to find out."

Laura slumped back in the bed. "I don't know."

"What don't you know?"

"Max. I mean, the wedding is due to be annulled soon."

"No one is going to sue you if you don't accept that challenge, you know."

"I know."

"*Do* you want to annul your marriage?"

She looked up into Kelly's eyes and shook her head. "No, I don't."

"Does Max want to?"

"I don't know. We haven't talked about it. In fact, he's studiously avoided it. I don't know *what* he's thinking."

"*I've* a pretty good idea. He doesn't want to annul the marriage and he doesn't want you to leave."

"You're guessing. How could you know?"

"Because I see how he is with you, and I see how you are with him. You're the same."

Laura narrowed her gaze. "For some reason you want me to stay with him, don't you?"

"I can tell you the reason if you haven't guessed it. I think you're good together. I think he's opened up a part of you which you've kept locked down for too long. I think you'll be happier *with* him, than without him."

Laura just looked at Kelly, stunned. "You've never said anything like that before."

"Because I didn't think I needed to. Because I wanted you to get there on your own."

"I have. At least I think I have."

"You don't have to run anymore, Laura."

"Is that what you think I've been doing?"

"No, it's what I *know* you've been doing. Do me a favor and talk it through with Max. It's time to make a few changes. Okay? Just talk with him, that's all I'm asking."

Laura nodded. "Okay. I will. I mean, I've been trying to figure out a way of bringing it up but with Mom and Dad nearby, we haven't had a minute on our own."

"Now's your moment so grab it with both hands. Starting with this challenge! Signal your interest and then accept it when he tells you what it is." Kelly leaned over to the keyboard and was about to signal Laura's interest but Laura took her hand and pulled it away and met her gaze before resolutely leaning forward and entering a smiley face with a thumbs-up.

"There, happy now?"

"Not yet." Kelly rose with a smug smile and walked toward the door. "But I will be." She opened the door and turned to her. "And so will you. Oh, and if you want anything just phone."

It wasn't until after Kelly had closed the door that Laura

realized the phone was over by the door, at least half-a-dozen steps away. "Kelly!" she called. But there was no response. She'd moved the damn phone on purpose to get Laura out of bed.

Annoyance gave Laura strength and she swung her legs off the bed. She quickly looked away from her legs which she could see had become skinnier beneath her pyjama pants. She gripped the side table and pushed herself to standing. She stood for a few seconds to let a slight dizziness pass and then took a step forward. Her foot rolled and her knees and legs took the strain, remembering what they had to do, despite the fact she'd grown weaker over the past months. But her heart was fine. All the doctors had agreed on that. She wouldn't make herself worse by moving. By exercising, she'd make herself better. She took another step and then another and grunted with relief when she gripped the table and picked up the phone. She dialed Kelly's number.

"And Kelly? I need physios. I need to get strong again."

MAX HAD BEEN as good as his word. The day of the challenge he posted what it was actually going to be.

"How the hell does he expect me to sled through the Southern Alps, and at night, too?" She pushed the laptop away. "It's impossible!"

"Nothing's impossible, Laura. You've proved that. Let's look through the challenge carefully, see if there's anywhere where we can tweak it."

"I *don't* tweak challenges," Laura replied darkly.

"You do now," Kelly said absently as she re-read it. "If you want to win this challenge, you'll have to."

"Give it here." Laura took the laptop and typed "ACCEPTED!!!" at the bottom.

Then she sat back and bit her fingernails. "I have no stamina! How the hell does he think I'm going to sled down a slope?"

"I guess you just sit there, do you? I don't know, I've never sledded. I've always sat and watched you from the sidelines."

"No! You have to move. You have to lean into the curves, you have to steer the damn thing. You have to move muscles which I don't have anymore." She chewed her lip as she thought it through. It would be suicide. She didn't have the strength. But there was a stubborn part of her that wouldn't give up. "I'm going to the gym."

"You've spent the morning with the physios."

"And I need to work harder, if I'm to survive this damn sledding descent."

Kelly helped her get dressed in her gym gear, which was now loose on her. She'd lost muscle. She'd have to work to get it back, that was if she didn't collapse in the process.

MAX HELD the door open for Laura who froze on the doorstep and looked back at him with panic written all over her face. It made him sad and determined at the same time.

"Max! I thought you told me no one would be here."

"Did I?" he grinned. "I must have lied."

But Laura didn't smile and Max didn't waver. "I can't face them, Max, I can't." She tried to step back but Kelly, who exchanged glances with Max, blocked the way. "They'll all be looking at me."

"You never found that a problem before."

"That was then. I'm not the same person."

He took her hands. Bravado wouldn't cut it. Maybe talking would. "You're exactly the same person, deep down. You're just a little more afraid now. And *you* know, as well as me, the only way to beat fear is to face it. You can't stay inside, away from people forever. Come on. Trial by fire. I won't leave your side." Still she didn't move. He suddenly remembered the words to her favorite David Bowie song. "We can be heroes..." he said.

"Just for one day," Laura whispered, finishing off the lyric. It did the trick. She nodded and he took her hand and opened the door.

"Laura!" The shouts came from all around. She smiled as she recognized some of the voices. They were all there, encouraging her, willing her on. Max hoped it would be enough.

"Hey!" She smiled and turned to them, letting go of Max's hand. He knew she didn't want people to think he was supporting her and he felt even more proud of her.

"How are you feeling, Laura?" called a photographer.

"Great, thanks. You?"

She chatted with the photographers and her fans and accepted their best wishes before moving on, guided by Max. They walked slowly across to the SUV and stopped. "So we're not sledding here at the Lodge, then?"

"No. Hop in the car and we'll get going."

"Hop?" She gave an adorable lop-sided grin. "Clamber ungracefully, more like."

Strange, Max thought, she seemed softer now. Her collapse might have knocked her for six, shaking the bravado with which she'd always faced life, but he felt, in some strange way, he could see the real her now. And he liked what he saw.

As she raised one leg on the high step to enter the vehicle, Max automatically reached out to help her. But one determined glance from Laura and he stepped away. A collective hush settled around the place, as if everyone was holding their breath, as Laura pushed off and stepped with apparent, but studied, ease into the vehicle. She sat down and looked around triumphantly. "What are you waiting for?"

The breath was released and a few cheers drifted on the cold icy air. Max smiled and closed the door behind her and jumped in the driver's seat.

"Better buckle up, the road's icy."

She whooped as he drove quickly but expertly along the gravel road and turned right, not toward Wanaka, but up to the top of the Crown Range road—New Zealand's highest main road.

They turned off the road up a snowy track and pulled in at a barn in which a half-dozen Alaskan Malamute dogs stood barking. She pressed her forehead against the windscreen, peering out across the white expanse. "Dog sledding?"

"Yeah. You didn't think I'd let you go on a normal sled now, did you?" He grinned and jumped out the car and opened her door for her. She stepped out carefully and walked up to the dogs and petted them. It was darker now and the sky above was a deep indigo, in which a sliver of moon didn't eclipse the light of the emerging stars. He turned on the sled's headlamp.

"Don't tell me." She looked up at him with flushed cheeks and bright eyes. "I'm driving one of these sleds."

"No way, lady. You can do that next year. For now, you're in there." He pointed to the sled he stood behind, a pile of fake furs ready for her. She burst out laughing and the laugh curled its way into his heart and gave an almighty tug. He had to swallow down the lump. This was what he wanted, wasn't it? For Laura to get better, to be happy again, to move on. The problem was with each passing day her growing strength would help her leave him. And that made him sadder than he thought possible.

. . .

LAURA HAD BEEN to many places and seen many things but nothing came close to that night run through the snow, high in New Zealand's Southern Alps—just her and Max, and six Malamutes.

The only sound was the dogs' feet, the runners of the sled slicing through the freshly fallen snow. The white of the surrounding land shone under the starlight and the breath of the dogs misted in the light of the sled's headlamp. And then there was what this challenge was all about—the wind on her face, teasing out her hair from beneath her hat, filling her lungs with its tingling freshness. By the time they reached the bottom, thirty minutes later, she felt the wind had blown something away from her, something she'd been wanting to leave behind for some time. Fear. And with it something else she'd been fighting with all her life had been released—her heart, her feelings. By the time Max helped her out of the sled, she knew exactly what she wanted. She took hold of his hand firmly, not through a physical need now, but an emotional one.

"How do you feel?" Max asked.

The expression in his eyes was kind, caring. But she didn't know if there was anything beyond that and there was no point in asking. What could she say? *Do you love me? Do you want to stay married?* Even if the answer was yes on both counts, she'd be leaving in a few days anyway. She'd agreed to return to the US with her parents to finish recuperating and also to spend some time with them and she couldn't change on her mind on that point.

No, she only had *this* moment, *this* evening to hold on to and experience something she'd never before experienced and she was determined that nothing should get in its way— least of all questions for which there were no satisfactory answers.

"I feel… good. *So* good. Thank you."

"My pleasure." He looked at her with an assessing gaze. "You look like your old self."

"Old self? No. I feel like my new self."

"And that's good? I quite liked the old Laura."

"It's most definitely good. I'm the same... yet different," she said with a small smile and a tilt of the head. Seems she hadn't left the old flirtatious Laura behind.

"Hm, sounds interesting."

She touched his cheek with her gloved hand. It was as close as she could get to him but it wasn't close enough. "Take me away from here, and I'll show you exactly how interesting it is."

He didn't reply, but gripped her hand with his and they walked through the crisp snow back to the waiting car.

ONCE BACK AT THE LODGE, Max, for once lacking in patience with the waiting crowds, texted Chelsey who emerged from the main building and dealt with the public, allowing Max and Laura to enter the building unseen. His grip on her hand hadn't lessened its hold as they walked through to his study, where a fire was roaring. He switched on a side light and she looked around.

"I haven't been in here before. It's very..." she grinned. "You."

"You mean there's nothing much here?"

"I mean," she said, stepping up to him and looking into dark eyes. "That what you see is what you get. That what is here, is what's important. Nothing else. You can trust a person like that."

He put his arms around her and pulled her to him. "You know you can trust me." She nodded, her cheek brushing the soft stuff of his shirt. She was about to speak but instead, stupid tears which never seemed far away now, sprung to her eyes.

"Laura?" He pushed away and lifted her chin. He frowned. "Are you crying?"

She tried to pull away but it suddenly felt impossible to hide anything from those dark penetrating eyes. She lifted her chin instead. "Yes." A hot tear tracked down her cheek.

"Why? Have I done something wrong?"

She swallowed. "Yes. You haven't kissed me yet."

He didn't need any further encouragement and his lips met hers in a kiss which was full of repressed need, and sent any lingering doubts about her intentions flying into the ether. For once she didn't fight it. Instead their bodies came close and she followed her instincts—instincts which had been too long been suppressed. Her hands found his hot skin, briefly contracting under her searching fingertips; her tongue found his, and her hips fitted against his, showing her that she wasn't the only one aroused.

When they pulled apart, both were breathless.

"Make love to me, Max," whispered Laura, in the husky voice of desire.

He groaned, a sound full of need and desire which made her melt further. "No way." He pulled back and gripped her shoulders.

She was shocked. She hadn't expected this response, especially when she had felt his body respond to her. "No?"

He gave a brief smile. "No. You've made it clear you're leaving, besides, you're a virgin." He opened his hands wide in reluctant defeat. "How can I?"

"I *am* a virgin, there's no disputing that. But it's not a permanent state, you know."

He looked at her for long, drawn-out seconds in which she could have sworn her breathing stopped. "No. You have to leave. You need to go back and heal your relationship with your family. You need to sort yourself out."

Disappointment bit deep but she'd be damned if she'd let it divert her from her course. "You think I'm not sorted?"

"I *know* you're not."

"Okay, I'll leave. But…"

He tilted up her chin. "Yes?"

"The annulment."

The word fell like a stone between them.

"What about it?"

"It doesn't have to happen… does it?"

"Nothing *has* to happen, one way or another. But… you know, I think it *does* have to be annulled. It was wrong. It all happened too fast, and for the wrong reasons. I want you to take this time to heal, to think and…"

"Yes?" She pounced on his hesitation, hoping there was some glimmer of hope.

"And… I don't want to hear from you, not during that time." He turned to the wintry view with a stony gaze.

It was like a stab to her still damaged heart. But maybe the scar tissue there was making it more resilient, because it made her more determined than ever to get what she wanted, despite the fact he wanted no future with her.

"Okay, but it still doesn't alter the fact that I want to go to bed with you." She pushed her fingers up through the short hair that grew above his collar, sweeping up into the longer hair before swirling her finger around in it and pulling it, trying to get him face her. He resisted though and continued to look out the window. She let her finger slip through his hair. He was like the mountains outside—immovable. She had the weird sense that she could only have the same connection with him, as the very mountains—could play, admire, but ultimately not affect them. The thought panicked her.

"Are you ignoring me, Max?"

He snorted. "That's pretty hard to do, Laura. I've seen people cheer you on, I've seen people laugh and talk to you, I've seen them react in all different ways, including anger, but I haven't seen anyone able to ignore you."

"*You* are."

"Laura. I want you to go."

Time seemed to stand still as they stood looking at each other. She'd read about heart aches, heard about them in love songs, but had never believed them to be real. Not until that moment. Looking at his eyes—boring into hers with an intensity she'd come to need—at his lips, opening as if to speak, as if to kiss, as if to stop her. But they didn't. Instead the details of his face became blurry until all she could see was his outline, obliterating the light, contrasting sharply to the cold white outside the window. Dark, light. Need, emptiness. Hope, despair. Being with Max was like standing before a fire—anything else felt cold and empty. Only *with* him was there enough heat to survive. But she knew about survival, didn't she?

Using more willpower than she'd ever done before she took a step behind her, toward the door. She had to close her eyes to tear them from his. She only opened them when she passed through the door and into the empty hallway. Cold. Just as she thought. She walked carefully along the corridor, measuring every step as a test of her strength, and as a distance from him.

It took all of Max's self-discipline to resist following Laura. If she'd hesitated, if she'd come to him again and kissed him, he didn't think he'd have been able to let her go. He'd have made love to her as she'd asked him to do. But she'd gone and, instead, he closed his eyes and tried to imprint every detail of her lovely face in his mind.

Tomorrow she'd be out of his life... *out of his life...* he kept repeating, in an effort to keep himself focused on reality. And that was exactly how it should be. She'd explained how she needed to return home and, on one level, he understood. Pity his heart didn't comprehend as easily as his brain. Just one sign from Laura now and his brain would have handed control to his heart.

Suddenly his laptop dinged. He twisted it round to face him, stabbed at a few keys and froze, his eyes narrowing as he re-read the challenge. The very *private* challenge. To him. Alone.

He pushed it away, as if it were a cobra about to strike, and stepped away. He stared at nothing, his mind full of the image of Laura leaving the room. The challenge said nothing of the future, only a demand for now and it was a challenge he could no longer refuse.

He rapidly typed his response and closed the laptop, turned off the light and walked out the door, towards Laura's room.

LAURA STOOD by the closed door, dressed only in her robe, and waited for Max to arrive. She heard him walk down the corridor and she opened the door before he had a chance to knock.

"Max," she breathed, her quiet, uncertain voice lost in the thickly carpeted hallway. He stood silhouetted against the subdued hall lighting. She stood back. "Come in."

He didn't move. "Are you sure?"

She nodded, suddenly not knowing what she thought. All she knew was what her body was telling her to do, and it seemed her brain had no power over that. "Sure, I'm sure."

He nodded thoughtfully and walked past her as she held the door open for him. She stood, hands pressed behind her against the door and watched him prowl around the room, like some animal scenting its prey. *Her?*

He stopped suddenly. "Tell me, Laura, what is it exactly you want?"

"Didn't I make that clear in the challenge?"

"No. You wanted me to come here, now. What for? I need you to be clear."

She opened her mouth to speak but no words emerged. She swallowed and cleared her throat. "I want you." She grimaced. Now she sounded too loud, as if she'd shouted the words at him. She sucked in a breath, trying to control the overwhelming feeling that she was about to stuff this up— her one and only chance to experience the love of which she'd never dared dream. "I want you to make love to me, Max." She uttered his name with an emotional twist in her voice which had the effect of shattering the reserve on his face.

"Laura!" He exhaled her name. "Are you sure?"

She nodded, not trusting herself to speak. She pressed her lips hard together to stop them from quivering and walked to him. He reached out and pushed his fingers through her hair and brought her head up to his. With both hands tangled in her hair he held her face, not as before, as if it were the most precious thing, but as if he wanted to lose himself in her. He pressed his mouth to hers with a soft grunt.

She felt as if her world had collapsed, that nothing existed except for the insistent caress of his lips on hers, inching into her soul, turning her body liquid and hot with desire. She'd been scared she wouldn't know what to do but she found her hands knew exactly where to go—molding over the contours of his chest, before sweeping up to his neck where she laced her fingers together, as if afraid he'd pull away. But, as he deepened the kiss, she realized there was only one thing to do—surrender. He wasn't going anywhere and the act of giving control to someone else, especially someone who appeared to have only her satisfaction on his mind, was thrilling.

She relaxed in his arms and he took control, pressing his body against hers, his arms holding her tight. She might weaken, but he'd support her, he'd make sure she didn't fall. She practically melted into his arms. But it seemed he was still cautious because when he pulled away, there was a look of concern on his face.

"Are you okay? We can stop if you like."

"I don't like!"

"But—"

She stepped back and undid the tie of her robe. It fell open and his gaze roved over her body with an appreciation and anticipation that nearly undid her. Slightly awkwardly she smoothed down her practical, toweling robe. "Not designed to seduce, I'm afraid."

He raised an eyebrow. "You don't need any design," he said with a crooked smile. He stepped forward. "All you need is for me to"—he pushed the robe from her shoulders and it fell to the floor—"do this."

She gasped but the gasp was robbed as his mouth took control of her once more, not only her lips now, but lower, allowing her no more time to consider anything, only experience *everything*. And she wanted to remember every minute of her night with Max, because she knew the memories might have to last her the rest of her life.

MAX SHIFTED SLIGHTLY in his sleep and Laura kissed the inside of his arm on which she lay. Making love to Max had been different to what she'd imagined. She'd always thought it would be like eating something delicious—a more than pleasant sensation which was over before it had a chance to begin. Something yummy, something ephemeral, something fleeting.

Gently, so gently so as not to awaken him, she stroked her hand down his chest, over the springy hairs and left her hand to rest over his heart which rose and fell with a rhythm which felt like her own. Fleeting? There was nothing fleeting about this. So where did that leave her?

Laura looked out the window at the snow clouds which swept darkly across the night sky, obliterating the stars. Thick snowflakes slapped against the glass, rested a few seconds, before their complexity broke down, combining, and slithering down the window pane, coming to rest in U-shaped drifts on the frame. It was mesmerizing. The minutes turned into hours as Laura lay awake, her burning eyes seeing more in the darkness than she'd ever seen before. The snow passed and the sky opened up again, visible above the small drifts which clung icily to the windows.

It was as if her thoughts and feelings were attuned to the sky, first shadowy, and then, as daylight approached, becoming clear.

It was only when she rose and looked out the window, toward the front of the lodge, that she saw it. The antique lantern was working. It shone its lone light into the slowly lightening world, signalling a welcome for everyone, a light to guide home anyone who had lost their way.

Suddenly *everything* had become very clear.

MAX LAY WITH EYES CLOSED, listening to the sound of Laura moving quietly around the room as she gathered her things together. She was going to leave, just slip away because she was right, there *was* nothing left to say.

She was going; he was staying. But still, as he listened intently to each sound she made—from her slow but clumsy movements as she tried, but failed, to be quiet—a lingering hope remained. It was only when he heard the clink of something metallic being placed onto an ornamental dish beside the bed, that the hope faded.

He held his breath, waiting to see what she'd do next. She hesitated and then walked to the door, opening it and closing it slowly so as not to disturb him. But she misjudged the door and it banged into place.

He immediately opened his eyes and stared into the breaking gray light. A quick scan of the room showed she hadn't left anything behind. She must have packed the previous night. She'd been prepared.

Something closed in his heart, then. He rose and entered the shower, turning it to cold—the same cold as the snow that fell outside the window. He didn't want warmth, he didn't want any attempt at comfort. There was none to be had. What he wanted was something to take the pain away, and if he couldn't do that, something to distract him from the pain he felt at the loss of her. Only then, when the cold traveled through his skin, driving into his muscles, into his bones, did he feel any element of rest. He allowed the numbness to fill him, his brain, his heart, his lungs. He'd done the right thing. He'd had to let her go, cut contact with her, because she wouldn't have done it and she needed to. It was the only way for her to really heal—not just physically, but emotionally, too. She'd wanted to try sex, he'd obliged. It was nothing more than that—on her part anyway.

He quickly dressed and went to work in his office. He didn't turn on the TV, or the computer, and had no inclination to check Twitter. He focused on nothing but work. And, as soon as the chairlift was open he took his skis and went to the top of the ski run. There he stayed for some time, looking around at the majesty of the mountains, which suddenly seemed insignificant compared to his feelings for Laura.

It was only after he'd watched the small cavalcade of cars drive carefully down the snowy road, that he'd skied down the mountain, expertly cutting through the fresh snow of the difficult run, the cold air stinging his face, cauterizing his lungs, and causing him sufficient pain to distract him from his other pain.

12

"LAURA'S BACK, SHE'S WELL, BUT IS SHE
READY FOR HER NEXT CHALLENGE?"
@TELLTALEGIRL #LAURA'SRETURN

Three months later...

*L*aura had done what he'd asked and hadn't contacted him. And he hadn't looked back. He'd thrown himself into his work. His life *was* his work. Hadn't it always been?

But it hadn't stopped him watching her transformation on the internet—from the YouTube "It Girl" who always accepted every challenge, to someone lower key, someone who posted more thoughtful comments, someone who'd stayed put in her community with her family, building bridges, making herself whole again. And he was happy for her. But less happy for himself.

Especially now. He glanced at the unopened email from Laura's solicitor. She hadn't even bothered to email him directly about it. It was what Max had feared—what had driven him into his work with almost desperate energy— she'd grown, but she'd grown away from him.

His hand hovered over the key to open the email but the tight knot inside in which he'd wrapped his feelings all those months ago threatened to unravel. He pushed his chair away from the desk as if retreating from something dangerous. It was business. That's all it was. Laura had grown so far away from him that she'd reduced their relationship to business. So he'd get Chelsey to handle it.

He walked through the Lodge to Chelsey's office. The place was busier than ever, thanks to all the publicity his marriage had brought him and his business. They'd been able to renovate and rebuild some of the older parts of the Lodge, and make it into the place he'd always envisaged it being. What he hadn't imagined was how empty he'd feel. Even the early spring buds on the cherry trees stirred the pain he always carried, emphasizing as they did, how much time had elapsed since he'd seen Laura.

He opened the office to see the now usual signs of activity. They'd taken on more staff to cope with the extra work and the place was humming. Chelsey sat in one corner talking on the phone, as immaculate and professional as ever. He stood in front of the picture window looking out at his, and his family's creation, as he listened to her end of the phone call.

"No problem, sir. Our chef will ensure the wedding dinner is exactly as you describe." She paused. "Yes, we look forward to seeing you then." She finished the call, and placed the phone on the desk. "Ha! Another wedding." She raised a satisfied eyebrow. "Seems we're the go-to place for weddings now. Everyone wants a 'Laura and Max' wedding."

Max's heart sunk a little lower. He hadn't thought it could fall any further.

"What's up?" asked Chelsey, leaning back in her chair and eyeing him with that penetrating way she had. "Bothered by the fact it's a 'Max and Laura' wedding?"

Max didn't dignify the question with an answer. "I... have

to go somewhere this morning. Deal with my emails, will you?"

"Where are you going?"

Max huffed an irritated sigh. "I have an appointment." He leaned on the desk in what he hoped was an assertive fashion. "Not that it's any of your business."

"Actually it is." She checked her computer screen diary. "And no, you don't."

"I don't have time for this." He walked toward the door.

"Max!"

He hesitated, hand on the door handle. "What?"

"Is everything okay?"

It was her softer tone which made him turn around. He tried to smile but he suspected, by her lack of response, that he hadn't succeeded. "Sure. Why wouldn't it be?"

She rose from her chair, came over to him, and placed her hand on his arm. "Maybe because you've had your heart broken for the first time in your life?"

"I don't need this, Chelsey. All I need is for you to deal with my emails. Okay?"

"You can't keep running from it, Max. You have to deal with it."

Max grunted in exasperation. "Why do I surround myself with women who never answer a direct question and who don't rest until they've interrogated me over every decision I make?"

Chelsey looked strangely sad and awkward. "I'm afraid there's nothing you can do about that. Because you see, Max Connelly, you're one of the good guys and whoever you let close, can't help caring for you."

Max instantly thought of Laura. "Not everyone, Chelsey, not everyone."

It was only when he stepped outside and was walking to his car that Chelsey's expression filtered through his own concerns. He stopped briefly and closed his eyes. He'd never wanted to hurt Chelsey. He'd thought she'd moved on. Maybe she had. Maybe, he thought as he continued to the car, she cared for him in a sisterly way. He hoped so. Either way what he'd said to her was true. He had to be somewhere, alright—*anywhere* but here.

~

It was late by the time Max returned to the Lodge. Despite the lateness of the hour, the office light was still on. He hesitated outside, fingered his phone which he'd been ignoring all afternoon, and went inside.

Chelsey was on the phone. She looked up as soon as he entered. "I'll call you later. Max has turned up." She tossed the phone down and turned to Max, hands on hips. "Why haven't you been answering my messages, my calls? Max! It's not on! You leave here without telling anyone where you're going and expect us to carry on as if nothing's happened. This is a business. *Your* business—"

He held up his hand to make her stop. "I know, I know. I'm sorry. I needed to get away for a few hours."

"It wouldn't be anything to do with that email you received from Laura's lawyers this morning, would it?"

He shrugged. "Why would it? Only another business email."

"Only another business email," Chelsey repeated as she walked to the laptop. "And I assume you believed it to be about the annulment of your marriage."

"Of course. That's what we planned."

"Well, you know, Max, what they say about the best laid plans…"

"So, you've dealt with it?"

"No, I haven't. It's not for me to deal with."

"I asked you to deal with it," he said, unable to prevent anger from creeping into his tone.

She folded her arms and looked at him squarely. "I've known you a long time and I've never seen you like this before."

"Like what?" he muttered, turning around. Chelsey was too damned perceptive.

"Like a lovelorn teenager."

He shot her a filthy look. "Don't be ridiculous."

"Okay a lovelorn man. Max, you might fool Laura, you might fool your family, but you don't fool me." She stepped away from the desk and went toward him. "You," she said, tapping her finger on his chest, "need to sort yourself out. And the sooner the better."

Suddenly all the pretense fell away. What was the point? He shook his head, full of despair. "I've been dreading this moment. I knew it was coming, but…"

"But you'd hoped she'd come to the end of the three-month 'no contact' period—which *you* instigated, may I remind you—and decide to stay married. To a man who'd told her to leave."

"Maybe… something like that."

She sighed and went to the laptop, pressed a few buttons so its contents was beamed onto the wall usually used for presentations. Then she took a step back and folded her arms. "Read that."

Max had no idea why Chelsey should have suddenly decided to ram the point home that his marriage had always been fake, that he'd fallen in love despite that, and that it had now come to the point where it had dissolved into nothing, as if it had never happened.

"Read!" said Chelsey. But it wasn't her imperative tone which made him look up at the screen. It was something else.

Chelsey's whole face was alight with amusement. "Read," she repeated, more softly.

He turned to the screen on which a letter from Laura's solicitor was projected. He scanned it, noted the formal wording but his eyes refused to move beyond a sentence, encased in the legalese.

"Laura McKinley requests the honor of your hand in marriage."

"What?" He turned in bewilderment to Chelsey.

"What do you mean, 'what'?" Chelsey said, doubling over with laughter. She stood up and wiped her tears. "It's a proposal of marriage, Max! Laura wants to marry you, in the top meadow. Next month."

"But our marriage hasn't been annulled yet!"

"And it doesn't look as if she wants it to be either. So, what do you say?"

Max smiled and shook his head. Then he looked back at the words, suddenly doubtful, suddenly not believing such a miracle could happen. "And you're sure this isn't someone's idea of a joke?"

"Sure, I'm sure. I've been in touch with Kelly who assures me Laura has been waiting for the three months to be up. But when it happened she was scared you didn't want her because you hadn't contacted her."

"I was waiting for *her*. It was up to *her*."

Chelsey rolled her eyes. "You guys! So… what are you going to do?"

Max didn't answer but walked across to the laptop and typed out a one word reply and sent the email. He rose with a grin and rolled back on his heels, hands in his pockets, feeling the wedding ring which Laura had returned to him all those months ago. "Well," he said to Chelsey. "What are you waiting for? You've another wedding to organize."

~

OUTSIDE THE QUEENSTOWN LODGE, the avenue of cherry trees swayed in the spring breeze, shedding their abundant blossoms over the gray-white stone-flagged driveway.

Last time she'd been here, the bare branches of the cherry trees had been white with snow. Laura couldn't help remembering looking down on them from the upstairs bedroom, watching the snow collect and become heavy on their boughs, the night she'd made love with Max. It seemed every moment of that night was etched in her memory. And now, seeing the trees which had borne witness to that night, made her feel she was home again.

She smiled to herself as her gaze rested on the lantern— its light muted in the daylight, but symbolic of what Max and the lodge meant to her. Home. That was something she'd been running from for what seemed forever. Who'd have thought she'd find it thousands of miles away from the place of her birth, in the mountains, with a man who was as crazy as she was?

"Laura!" called Kelly. "Please, just a little makeup? Think of the photos," she pleaded.

"No photos. I don't want photos. And, no." She smiled at the makeup artist, who'd just finished Kelly's and Chelsey's nails. "Really, no makeup."

"Well, if that's how you want to play it..." said Kelly.

"It is." She smoothed down her white summer dress, its simplicity alleviated only by a lace trim and flirty cut. She peered into the mirror. She didn't seem to have any problems looking at herself now. She smiled at her reflection and shook her hair. It fell back into place, unhampered by either hair spray or styling gel. Just straight with a bit of a kink in it so it flicked away from her face. It was shorter than she'd worn it last time she'd been in New Zealand. She'd decided on the short, choppy bob, as a statement of her new beginning. The child had gone; long live the woman.

A woman who had never been more nervous. "Do you think my hair's okay?"

"Since when have you cared about your hair?" asked Kelly, giving it a brief glance.

"Since I'm about to renew my wedding vows. That's when."

Kelly sighed and gave her a critical look. "I guess the best you could say is it looks natural. Chelsey, what do you think?"

Chelsey finished persuading the make-up artist that the bride really didn't want to wear any makeup. "Darling, you could wear a beehive or a onesie and Max would still think you looked fabulous. Although"—she glanced at Laura's tanned arms and shoulders and low top—"on second thoughts, I think he'd be less pleased with a onesie."

Chelsey's phone rang and she walked out the room, leaving Kelly alone with Laura.

"Don't forget your shoes," said Kelly, indicating the flat ballet pumps Laura had decided on.

Laura glanced at the neglected shoes and frowned.

Kelly came and sat down and slipped her arm around Laura and gave her a hug. "What's the matter? Aren't you happy?"

"I don't know. I think so. I mean, of course I am. Oh Kelly, am I doing the right thing?"

"What do you mean? You love Max, don't you?"

"Of course I do. You *know* I do. Not a day, or night, has passed when he hasn't been front and center of my thoughts. I love him, like I've never loved anyone else. I love him like he's a part of me. I love him like, together we'll be better, like he'll make my life bigger if I'm with him."

"Then you've answered your question."

"But does he love me?"

"He told you so, didn't he?"

"Yeah, right before he told me to leave and not contact him for three months."

Kelly waved her hand dismissively. "Phh! That? That's not about him not loving you! That's about him being as daft as you and giving you the space to think things through." Kelly leaned into the mirror and smudged away a dab of errant mascara before sitting back and checking the results critically. "Besides, he agreed to all of this, didn't he?"

"Yes, but…" Laura rose and paced across the room before turning and pacing back again.

Kelly sighed. "But what?"

Laura stopped pacing. "But maybe I should have seen him, talked to him before the ceremony. Maybe I shouldn't have relied so much on what Rachel told me."

"About how Max cried like a baby in the hospital? Of course you should. It proved that whatever he might say or not say, he adores you. Laura, don't worry! He loves you and you love him and you'll live happily ever after." The phone rang and Kelly answered it.

Laura paced to the window and looked out. Was Kelly's glib response correct? Laura knew she loved Max. With each passing day that knowledge had grown.

When she'd first returned to the US, she'd thrown herself into becoming strong physically. Thanks to the physiotherapy and the gym, she was now stronger than ever. Thanks to her parents and friends she was stronger emotionally.

During the long evenings out on the porch of their San Francisco home, she and her parents had talked like they'd never talked before. Their lives had been unraveled and opened up for inspection. It had been hard for all of them to talk over what had happened to Laura—her illness, her subsequent relentless traveling, her fame—but talk they had, until they'd finally lain to rest the old ghosts which had haunted their relationships. And once the wound had been opened it had healed cleanly.

Now, as Laura looked out to the garden, where Jim Connelly stood talking to her father, and her mother looked slightly bemused as she listened to some story of Amber's, Laura finally felt she'd arrived. Max had been right. She *had* needed that time to herself to put her life in order. She owed it to him that, when they did get together, it would be for the right reasons.

Her breath caught in her throat, and she clutched her necklace as Max came up to his father and put his arm around him. Seems she wasn't the only one healing family rifts. Jim's face widened into a beam as he continued to talk to Laura's father who stood quietly listening.

It was the first time she'd seen Max since her arrival early that morning. His hair was longer. Somehow it shocked her. She'd imagined him a certain way over the last three months, and he'd changed. Stupid, she chided herself. Nothing stood still, not ever. She'd changed her hairstyle after all. And that was only a part of it. Fear gripped her stomach. If she'd changed, then so, maybe, had he. And if so, how? Had his feelings toward her changed at all?

As her traitorous thoughts niggled at her, her hungry eyes sought every detail of his appearance, from his open-necked shirt—at her request, she sighed at the thought of his chest, warm against her lips—to his casual stone chinos. He was tanned from the hot New Zealand sun, and, as he looked over, toward something or someone standing near her window, she could see his intense tawny eyes. She swayed and gripped the stone windowsill. There would be hot times, tempestuous times, but there would be a lot of loving, a lot of fun, and ultimately, a future she couldn't be without.

The door opened and Kelly popped her head round. "Ready?"

Laura didn't turn around immediately, but continued looking at Max. "Ready? Definitely."

IT WASN'T EXACTLY as Max had imagined as he looked around the grassy mountainside above which snow still lingered. Snowdrops and early mountain flowers trembled and swayed in the fresh breeze. Beneath the lone tree stood a marriage celebrant and a small gathering of people. A quick scan showed that Laura had yet to appear. His nerves hitched up a notch.

He knew she'd arrived that morning but hadn't seen her. Despite her withdrawal from the limelight, she couldn't avoid publicity. There was a buzz around the place since her arrival which had nothing to do with his nerves and all to do with Laura. He reckoned it would always be that way.

He went and spoke to his father, his brothers and sisters before taking his place. This wasn't a wedding. It was a renewal of vows. But it *was* the real wedding. There was no sign of Laura's entourage. Then he heard that laugh and he turned to see Laura and Kelly walking up the hill. Laura radiated sunlight. There were bright flowers in her hair and she wore a long flowing dress and was barefoot. She waved to Max and all of Max's fears and doubts vanished. He was only aware of her, her unwavering gaze fixed on him, her smile answering his.

She came closer, and her hand reached out and clasped his. This was real, then, he thought, as they both turned, unable to tear their eyes from one another.

"You're here," she said with a smile. "I wasn't sure you'd come."

"It's not every day I receive a proposal of marriage from my wife."

He brought her hand to his lips and kissed it. The wind blew her hair into her face. She pushed it behind her ears. She wasn't wearing any makeup, just as he liked, just as she liked.

The music stopped and the marriage celebrant began to speak. Max was hardly aware of what was being said, only that Laura was here, beside him, holding his hand, and looking healthier and stronger than he'd ever seen her. It was as if a light had been turned on in his heart. The marriage celebrant coughed and both Max and Laura looked at her.

"Laura," prompted the celebrant.

"Oh, right!" Laura laughed.

The small group of friends and family who surrounded them burst out laughing.

"Max," she said squeezing his hand. "This has come as something of a surprise, I know, but there are things I want to say, with everyone who is important to us around us." She took a deep breath. "Our last marriage was a sham. And I'm sorry about that. I'm not saying I regret it, because I don't. After all, without it, we wouldn't be here." She bit her lip. "But it was a sham nonetheless. And I want to start afresh. I want this ceremony to be special, not just for us, but for all our loved ones."

Max looked around at his beaming family and friends. "It *is* special." He pushed a stray lock of hair back from her face. "*You've* made it special."

"When I'm with you, I *feel* special." She tried to rein in the soppy grin which she knew was forming, and concentrate. "I told you once that you should simply take my love, that it would be easier for us both. And you said—"

"That your heart, your love, was yours to give. I couldn't

take it from you. I'll never take anything from you that's not freely given."

"I see that now. I understand. You gave me space to understand and that's yet another reason why I love you, and always will. And I want to say to you now, all those things which we didn't say last time, which we can say now, because I—"

"We," interrupted Max.

"Because *we* mean them. Max, I pledge to love you and be faithful to you, for better or worse, *forever*. Max?"

Max hadn't prepared anything. He'd wondered what form the ceremony was going to take, but it seemed informal was the order of the day. Just as well.

"Laura, I think I loved you the instant I set eyes on you. It probably took me a couple of weeks to know for sure and from that moment on, I've been yours and I want you to be mine. But I know you needed space to recover, to get well again, to become strong again and you have. And now you're here, I want our families and friends to know that I adore you, and will always do my best to make you happy."

There was a general sniffing and clearing of throats by their families and friends before the celebrant spoke again. But the words were lost on Max and Laura who had said all they needed to say to each other

He bent down and kissed her gently, before pulling away, and retrieving the ring from his pocket.

"Laura, with Dad's blessing I give you my mother's ring. If she were here, she'd have more than approved of what we're doing today. Her life was about love and this ring"—he held it up in the sunlight—"bears testament to that."

He pushed the ring onto her finger which now went smoothly, her body no longer rebelling against her ailing heart. She stood on tiptoes and kissed him. He caught her in his arms and the kiss deepened. Finally they pulled away and were aware of everyone cheering and clapping.

"I don't think we're going to be in this marriage on our own," murmured Max.

"No, we've our families—"

"Friends–"

"And let's not forget Telltale Girl!"

"Did you ever discover Telltale Girl's identity?" Max asked, as they walked through the wild flower meadow to the Lodge.

Laura shook her head. "Uh-uh. But whoever she is, *wherever* she is, she's one true friend. Like Kelly, over there." Laura laughed. "Even if she is glued to her phone. No doubt telling the world about the wedding."

"Come on, the sooner the dinner is over with, the sooner the family's gone to bed happy—"

"Then we can go to bed—"

"And be *very* happy," said Max with a suggestive raised brow.

But they hadn't progressed far before someone passed Laura her phone. "She's done it again! Telltale Girl has commented on your second wedding."

Laura took the phone and glanced at the message:

"The lovely Laura's second wedding to the handsome Max went without a hitch, so Telltale Girl understands. And Telltale Girl is especially touched to hear that Laura gratefully acknowledged Yours Truly for her encouragement into marriage. My reply to Laura is that Telltale Girl is truly ecstatic to see Laura happy again."

Laura laughed and was about to give the phone back before something struck her and she looked at the message once more. "The time! That's only thirty seconds ago." She looked up at the small group of people who had been the only witnesses to the wedding. "But no one here..." Her voice trailed off as she watched Kelly grin to herself and slip her phone back in her bag.

Kelly? Laura was stunned. Could her best friend really have begun this whole journey for Laura? Could she really have continued to prod and push Laura forward when she least wanted to? Could it have been Kelly who had made Laura face the future with a strength that she hadn't known she had, but which Kelly—aka Telltale Girl—obviously believed in?

Laura fingered the heart locket her best friend had given her when she was recovering from rheumatic fever. Kelly gave her a friendly wave and a warm smile. Of course it was her. Who else would want her to be truly happy, who else would make her face her emotional side—the part of her she'd been avoiding her whole adult life? Who else but her dearest friend? And she'd repay her. She'd make sure, in turn, that Kelly found someone like she'd found Max.

"Laura!" Max turned from talking to his father, his hand still firmly encasing hers. "Are you ready?"

"Are you kidding? I think I've been waiting my whole life for this moment."

"Strange. Dad said much the same thing about me."

"What did he say?"

"That I've been treading water, but that now the journey's about to begin."

"I think he's right," she said, falling into step beside Max, while the people she loved walked beside and behind them, down the flower strewn meadow, ringed with mountains, to her new home below.

It had only just begun alright.

EPILOGUE

"I KNOW WHEN I'M NO LONGER NEEDED!
BUT WHAT'S NEXT FOR TELLTALEGIRL?
ANOTHER PROJECT, MAYBE?"
@TELLTALEGIRL #THEEND

"*T*hat's it! Eighteen thousand feet! Ready?"

Laura nodded and passed her oxygen mask to the crew member. She gave the thumbs up to the pilot and jumped. The sudden rush of air nearly winded her. She fell through the air at over a hundred miles per hour in an ecstasy of fear, awe and excitement. She'd parachuted many times but always solo, and never this high. She looked around and suddenly Max came into vision. He maneuvered himself, and reached out and grabbed her hand.

She swung around and took his other hand. For thirty seconds, there was only her and Max, their bodies flat against the wind, holding onto each other as the earth rushed rapidly towards them. She looked down at the world which was getting bigger with each passing second, and marveled at the beauty of the land below them—the distant mountains, the bright blue flashes of lakes, snaking rivers and the towns like toys nestled into the folds of the valleys. Then she looked back into his eyes and saw another whole world of which she knew she'd never tire.

Then it was time. They separated and pulled their parachutes open and their hurtling descent was suddenly halted by the sheltering umbrella of silk overhead. Time slowed and they each steered themselves to better admire the beauty of the land below them and each other. In the form of a graceful dance, they descended and returned to earth. Max landed first and then Laura, who ran straight into his arms.

"Okay?" he asked.

"That was fantastic!"

"No cameras around to witness the highest group skydive in the world," said Max as he swept his knuckles down her cheek and lifted her chin. "Does it lose some of its thrill, having only me here to witness it?"

She enjoyed any opportunity to tease and so assumed a thoughtful expression. "You know, maybe you're right. Maybe I should have tweeted about it. And maybe I should invite people into other aspects of my life... more personal ones. I've heard an audience can do wonders for one's sex—"

Before she could finish Max growled and pulled her hard against him and kissed her possessively, leaving her under no illusion as to his opinion on the matter.

Eventually she pulled away with a sigh. "Or maybe not."

"I should think not. So... where to next? Back home and back to work?"

"Uh-uh," she shook her head. "I want to do that again."

"The jump or the kiss?"

"First one, and then the other."

Before Max could reply, Laura nestled into his arms and made it quite clear which would come first. The silk of the parachutes billowed and settled all around them, hiding their kisses from the world. And that was just how she liked it.

∾

Dear Reader,

Thank you for reading *Yours to Give,* the first in my **Lantern Bay** series. I hope you enjoyed it! Reviews are always welcome—they help me and they help prospective readers decide if they'd enjoy the book.

The next book in the series is *Yours to Treasure,* featuring Rachel Connelly and Zane Black, ex professional rugby player. An excerpt follows.

If you're new to my books and would like to know more about some of the characters you've met in *Yours to Give,* why not check out my **Mackenzies** series? The last book in the series, Summer at the Lakehouse Café, features Lizzi (Max's sister) and Pete.

If you'd like to know when my next book is available you can sign up for my new release e-mail list via my website —sophiehaydon.com.

Happy reading!

Sophie

YOURS TO TREASURE

BOOK 2, LANTERN BAY—RACHEL AND ZANE

Celebrity chef Rachel Connelly has it all—brilliant career, friends and family. But, at 28, she wants a relationship with a man who doesn't consider using compromising photos of herself to be a career move, and who doesn't believe it's his manly duty to make love to as many women as possible. After one failed love affair too many, she

realizes she needs to sort herself out and there's only one way to do that. Return to the place where it all began—Belendroit, her family home—and uncover the secrets surrounding a decision she made ten years earlier.

Ever since his birth mother uprooted him from his happy childhood, ex-professional rugby player Zane Black, has been determined to succeed—but only on his terms. He's principled, he's focused, and he refuses to compromise on anything. Particularly when it comes to protecting the two things in the world which are most important to him—his loved ones and his people. But when he has to hurt one loved one in order to protect another, his black and white world shatters...

EXCERPT

Rachel Connelly placed her jandal-clad feet either side of the dried arrangement which her father liked to call a 'dormant' camellia shrub, and gripped it as close to the base as possible. She gave a small tug to test. Nothing. This sucker was tougher than it looked. She took a deep breath and shifted her weight from foot to foot, gaining a more secure stance. Then she gripped it lower down and gave a short, sharp tug. It came away easily—too easily, Rachel thought with a small cry, as she found herself flat on her backside on the grass.

"Hey!" a voice called through the woods. "Are you okay?"

She turned to see runner's shoes and legs—strong, brown, hairy legs—running up to her through the small copse of trees which lay between the house and the road. She twisted onto her stomach and looked up, at the same time as the knees bobbed down and a concerned face came into view. A strangely familiar face.

"I'm fine," she said, trying, but not succeeding, to place the face. Another glance at the face and the familiarity receded. She definitely didn't know this man.

"Here." He reached out and placed a large hand under her upper arm. "Let me help you up."

Before Rachel could reply, the hand lifted her as if she were a feather. She definitely *wasn't* a feather.

"Oh! Well, thank you." She slowly looked up, past running shorts and a sleeveless t-shirt which revealed a body that was built. *Really* built. She didn't know whether her gasp was audible or not, but by the looks of his grin, she suspected it was.

He ducked his head to inspect her face. "You sure you're okay?"

"Yes, it was only a tumble." She waved around the dead shrub she was still holding, unable to move her gaze from his. "It came away easier than I thought."

He looked at it with a smile. "It would do. It's been dead these past couple of years. Like much of these woods. I've been wondering when someone would do something about it."

"Ah, that someone is my father. And he's still not convinced anything needs doing."

"You're one of the Connellys, then?"

"Yes. Rachel Connelly."

He stuck out his hand. "Pleased to meet you. I'm Zane Black."

She frowned. The instant she'd seen him she'd thought she'd known him, but she didn't. His name wasn't familiar and she was sure she wouldn't have forgotten someone like him.

She took hold of his hand and it felt good—big, strong, and yet gentle. It didn't grip you as if it was trying to make you submit, trying to make you aware of how strong he was. There was obviously no need for that.

"Good to meet you, Zane. You live round here?"

"Yeah, in the next valley. Up from Ti Tahi Bay."

There was a small flutter in her stomach. *Ti Tahi*. It sent memories flooding back of the time when she was only barely out of childhood and anxious to become an adult—a sexual adult.

"Ti Tahi," she repeated.

"Yeah. It's up in the hills near here. It's a small community built around a meeting house. My ancestors have lived on the land for centuries. It's steeped in history."

You bet it is, she thought. Including mine. "Yes, I know where it is."

"You do? Have you met my family?"

"No. Never. At least I don't think I have." She'd only known the boy who'd taken her virginity. She'd never met his family.

"I've seen you before." He suddenly looked unsure, as if he suspected he'd said too much.

"Where?" Surely she wouldn't forget someone as striking as him?

He looked around as if hoping someone would rescue him. There was no one. He turned back to her. "Oh, around."

"You like cooking?" she asked. Most people recognized her from her shows.

He shrugged and looked even more confused if that was possible. "Why?"

"Just wondered… about where you might have seen me before."

"Ah," he said, but didn't elaborate.

"Rachel?" A voice came from the house behind them. She turned and saw her father, Jim Connelly, waving at her. "Amber's been trying to reach you on the phone!"

"Okay!" she called, retrieving the quietly vibrating phone from where she'd left it, perched on a mostly empty wheelbarrow. "Excuse me," she muttered to Zane. "Hello?" She half-turned away. "Amber! Hi! Yes, sure, I'll be at the café mid-afternoon at the latest. See you then." She smiled as Amber made kissing noises down the phone. She finished the call and glanced up to see a pair of interested eyes quickly look away.

"I'd better go," said Rachel. "Things to do... Places to go..." She smiled uncertainly, feeling uncomfortable standing so close to this giant of a man who was clad only in brief shorts and t-shirt, exposing dark skin and a muscled body. Stunning, she thought, trying to keep her gaze away from his body, and focused on his face. Trouble was, that was impressive, too, in an uncompromising kind of way.

"Sure." He grinned and his face lit up, softening his features and revealing perfect teeth. He looked like a different man. He took a few steps back and indicated the garden. "Go easy on the weeding."

She nodded, and tossed the dead shrub into the wheelbarrow, feeling unaccountably shy. He turned away and began to jog back to the road. "See you," said Rachel impulsively. Some urge made her want to say something more to him, to keep the connection going.

"Yeah." He turned and grinned again. "You will."

ALSO BY SOPHIE HAYDON

The Mackenzies

A Place Called Home

Secrets at Parata Bay

Escape to Shelter Springs

What you See in the Stars

Second Chance at Whisper Creek

Summer at the Lakehouse Café

Lantern Bay